The Case of
Italian Indigestion

A Josie and Chef Claire Sojourn

The Thousand Islands Doggy Inn Mysteries

B.R. Snow

I0628356

Website: www.brsnow.net
Twitter: @BernSnow
Facebook: facebook.com/bernsnow

Cover Design: Reggie Cullen

Other Books by B.R. Snow

The Thousand Islands Doggy Inn Mysteries

- The Case of the Abandoned Aussie
- The Case of the Brokenhearted Bulldog
- The Case of the Caged Cockers
- The Case of the Dapper Dandie Dinmont
- The Case of the Eccentric Elkhound
- The Case of the Faithful Frenchie
- The Case of the Graceful Goldens
- The Case of the Hurricane Hounds
- The Case of the Itinerant Ibizan
- The Case of the Jaded Jack Russell
- The Case of the Klutz King Charles
- The Case of the Lovable Labs
- The Case of the Mellow Maltese
- The Case of the Natty Newfie
- The Case of the Overdue Otterhound
- The Case of the Prescient Poodle
- The Case of the Quizzical Queens Beagle
- The Case of the Reliable Russian Spaniels
- The Case of the Salubrious Soft Coated Wheaten

The Whiskey Run Chronicles

- Episode 1 – The Dry Season Approaches
- Episode 2 – Friends and Enemies
- Episode 3 – Let the Games Begin
- Episode 4 – Enter the Revenuer
- Episode 5 – A Changing Landscape
- Episode 6 – Entrepreneurial Spirits
- Episode 7 – All Hands On Deck
- The Whiskey Run Chronicles – The Complete Volume 1
- The Whiskey Run Chronicles – The Complete Volume 2

The Damaged Posse

- American Midnight
- Larrikin Gene
- Sneaker World
- Summerman
- The Duplicates

Other Books

- Divorce Hotel
- Either Ore

To Jeff and Sharon

Musings While I Wander

Italy in October – 1

After several weeks of futile protest on my part, I got tired of being nagged by my best friends, Josie and Suzy, and finally agreed to create a food and travel blog. Josie and I have decided to take a couple of trips each year to study the cuisines of different countries and cultures. As a chef, it's important for me to keep learning to improve my historical understanding of food as well as stay on top of new trends. And what better way to do that than by traveling and immersing myself in local cultures and the daily lives of others who either cook for a living or just for their family.

As I said, Josie and Suzy thought it would be a great idea for me to share some of our travel experiences as well as interesting recipes people might like to try out at home. So, this is the first entry of *Musings While I Wander*. I like the title and am looking forward to sharing some thoughts and recipes with you. And the first several posts will deal with our trip to Italy.

Italy was the perfect choice for our first trip. As a chef, I'm familiar with the cuisine, and we offer several Italian dishes at our restaurant in Clay Bay. But Italy offers so many regional variations, I felt my skills and repertoire could be improved by doing a deep-dive into some of the subtle, yet distinct, variations from around the country. And the number of excellent wines produced here will undoubtedly expand our drinking expertise. I'm joking, of course. But after the two bottles of a 2005 Turriga we polished off last night at dinner, I'm already beginning to have my doubts.

We landed in Rome two days ago and spent most of our time seeing the sights. We toured the Vatican where we saw the Sistine Chapel and St. Peter's Square, explored the Forum and the Colosseum, visited the Trevi Fountain and a few other museums and galleries. It was a lot to cover in two days, but we made it through and spent whatever time was left eating and drinking.

Suzy would love this place, but she's home taking care of the Doggy Inn she and Josie run and taking care of our dogs. I already miss Al and Dente, my Golden Retrievers, and I know Josie is also missing Captain, her Newfie. But they're in good hands. In addition to all the dogs, Suzy is also responsible for taking care of herself because she is pregnant. At least she better be. If she's not, Josie and I are going to kick her butt. (And I know you're reading this Suzy, so you better pay attention to that last comment.)

Last night, we caught a flight from Rome to Milan, and this morning we're driving to Lake Garda. We'll be spending a week at a beautiful villa named La Bella Vita. That translates into The Good Life which is the perfect name for a place where we'll spend each day learning how to prepare various Italian specialties then spend the evening eating what we make.

I'll be doing the driving today, and Josie has agreed to navigate. It should be a leisurely, two-hour scenic drive. But last night we discussed the possibility of getting off the highway and taking a few back roads to get a better feel for the Northern Italy countryside. It could add an hour or two to our trip, but we have tons of time. And we travel well together, no small consideration when you're on the road and in constant contact with your traveling companion.

So, it's off to school for us.

I'll give you another update after we get settled in. But before I go, I'd like to share a delicious recipe with you that will definitely impress your family and dinner guests. We had it for lunch yesterday, and it was, as Suzy would have undoubtedly confirmed, a total knee-buckler.

It's called Cacio e Pepe, and it's simple, delicious, cheap to make, and doesn't take a lot of time to prepare. The name translates into 'cheese and pepper,' so if you aren't a fan of copious amounts of these two ingredients, you probably won't enjoy the dish. But if you are, think of the best macaroni and cheese you've ever eaten and double the memory. That's how good this dish is when it's perfectly prepared.

Cacio e Pepe

Serves 4. (Less if you've invited Josie to dinner.)
Ingredients

- 1 pound thick spaghetti
- 1 tablespoon salt

- 2 tablespoons freshly ground black pepper
- 1½ cups freshly grated Pecorino Romano (a)
- 1 cup pasta water (approximate)
- Splash of olive oil, if desired (b)

(a) Parmesan is an acceptable substitute, but if you decide to go that route, you won't technically be serving the traditional version. But it's still going to put a big smile on your face, so knock yourself out.

(b) I haven't found consensus on the inclusion of olive oil. Some folks say it's an essential ingredient. Others argue it's not included in the traditional recipe. My suggestion is to do what you want, and if anybody asks about it or gives you a hard time, tell them it's an old family recipe that has been around for generations, and your great grandma was never wrong when it came to food.

Instructions

- Bring a large pot of water to a boil. Add the salt. (Use a little less water than usual. This will create starchier water, something you need for the sauce to develop.) Cook your pasta until it's al dente. (The pasta will cook a little more when you're making the sauce, so don't overcook your pasta.)

- Drain pasta and put it into a large bowl. (Reserve a cup or so of the hot pasta water.)
- Working fast, add in 1¼ cups Pecorino Romano cheese immediately, reserving the remaining ¼ cup.
- Add in ½ cup of the pasta water and pepper. (If you're using the splash of olive oil, add it here.)
- Toss with tongs to allow the heat from the pasta and water to melt the cheese. Add remaining water in small amounts until the pasta is coated with a thick, creamy sauce. Again, no dawdling here. Work fast and stay focused.
- Serve hot sprinkled with remaining cheese and pepper to taste.

The WOW Factor

To dazzle your family and friends, try the simple addition of making a serving bowl out of cheese you can eat. Talk about cleaning your plate. (You'll need more Pecorino Romano than is mentioned in the above recipe so keep it in mind when shopping if you decide to add this step.) Also, if you decide to add this step, do the following before you start preparing the meal, or while you're waiting for your pasta water to boil.

- Spread 1/2 cup of Pecorino Romano in a thin layer on the bottom of a non-stick saucepan and cook on low to medium heat for three minutes, or until it becomes pliable.
- Keep a close eye on it the entire time.
- Remove the cheese sheet from the pan with a spatula.
- Place the cheese sheet on top of an inverted ramekin or small bowl and, if necessary, use your hands to fit the sheet to the shape of the object. (Be careful, it might be a bit hot in spots.)
- Let it cool, then flip it over. Viola, you've made a cheese bowl.
- Repeat the process for the number of people eating.
- When the pasta is ready to serve, use tongs to fold the pasta into the Pecorino Romano bowls. Serve immediately and enjoy!

Okay, that's it for now. I need to hit the road. Josie is standing in the doorway tapping her watch and patting her stomach.

A road trip through beautiful countryside with one of my best friends.

I can't wait. It should be a fun, relaxing way to start the day.

Chapter One

Chef Claire white-knuckled the steering wheel of the rental car as the Ferrari approached from behind and ended up inches behind the back bumper. The driver leaned hard on the horn, and she could hear the muffled string of expletives coming out of his mouth.

"Aren't you glad you can't speak Italian?" Josie said as she glanced over her shoulder at the car directly behind them.

"Actually, I think he's screaming at me in English," Chef Claire said, keeping a close eye on the Ferrari in the rear-view mirror. "What do you want me to do?" she yelled into the mirror.

The driver, finally out of patience, dropped back several feet then hammered the accelerator. The Ferrari screamed past them, barely, then disappeared from sight.

"The guy has got a death wish," Chef Claire said.

"Probably only for slowpoke tourists," Josie deadpanned.

9

"You want to drive?"

"Don't yell at me."

Chef Claire focused her glare on the winding stretch of road opening up in front of the car. She glanced over at Josie who was gripping the sides of her seat with both hands. Chef Claire slowed as she maneuvered the car through a series of S-bends then exhaled when the road straightened. But before she could completely relax, the road narrowed. Chef Claire shook her head in disbelief.

"I've seen wider bike paths. Are we still on the right road?" Chef Claire said.

"It's hard to tell," Josie said, studying the map in her lap. "I think so."

"It looks like we might be on somebody's driveway."

"The road's just narrow," Josie said. "Truck."

"What?" Chef Claire said, glancing over.

"Truck. Big truck."

Chef Claire glanced out the windshield, shook her head as she slowed and moved as far as she could to the side of the road. The truck rumbled by without giving them a second look. Chef Claire accelerated slowly but was soon dealing with another winding section of road. Josie felt the glare she was receiving but didn't make eye contact.

10

"Don't look at me. You're the one who wanted to get off the highway and take the scenic route."

"Only because you said you could read a map," Chef Claire said. "Why don't you use your phone?"

"I can't get any reception," Josie said, glancing out the window. "But it is a beautiful drive."

"I'll take your word for it."

"Don't be a grump," Josie said. "We should be able to get a look at Lake Garda soon."

"I need to get out of this car."

"It won't be long," Josie said, again studying the map. Then she frowned. "Uh-oh."

"What?"

"It's nothing. Oh, look. There's the lake."

"Where?" Chef Claire said, glancing out the driver-side window. "All I see are rocks and trees."

"Right over there," Josie said, pointing out her window. "It's beautiful."

Chef Claire took her eyes off the road long enough to sneak a peek. Then she glared at Josie.

"What's the matter?" Josie said, avoiding eye contact.

"The lake is on our right, Josie."

"Yeah, I see it," she said, deflecting. "Gorgeous, huh?"

11

"That means we're heading north on the western side of the lake. How the heck did that happen?" Chef Claire said, looking for a place to pull over. Unable to find a spot to do it safely, she kept driving. She checked the rear-view mirror then glanced at the map still sitting on Josie's lap. "Geez, Josie. You've got the map upside down."

"Oh, you noticed," Josie said with a shrug. "I don't know how I managed that."

"Probably because you were more focused on your sandwich," Chef Claire, finally spotting a place to turn the car around.

"And you weren't?" Josie said, raising an eyebrow.

"Yeah, when we were eating at the restaurant."

Josie shrugged it off.

"Great sandwich, huh?"

"Yeah, it was good," Chef Claire said, nodding as she entered another winding stretch. "I still can't believe you managed to eat two of them."

"I wanted one for the road. And driving around in circles always makes me hungry."

"Don't start," Chef Claire said.

The sandwich in question was a fresh ciabatta roll slathered with a young, spreadable Gorgonzola produced

12

locally along with salami and thick tomato slices sitting on a bed of arugula.

"I've never eaten soft Gorgonzola before," Josie said, then shrugged.

"Add it to the list of things you've never had before," Chef Claire said, accelerating as the road straightened.

"I can't believe the food here," Josie said, tightening her grip on her seat. "The Italians are amazing."

"Yeah, they certainly are. And so much of it is regionally-based," Chef Claire said. "I can't wait for cooking school to start."

"Slow down, Leadfoot," Josie said. "Or we might not make it to class."

"Just read the map," Chef Claire said.

They continued heading south on the western side of the lake, and after passing the towns of Moniga and Padenghe, they reached Desenzano del Garda at the southern end. Chef Claire parked, and they got out to stretch and read the directions they'd been given to La Bella Vita, the villa they would be staying at for the week.

"It says we take the road right behind us and head south for two miles," Josie said. "Sounds easy."

"Let me see those," Chef Claire said, reaching for the directions.

"O ye, of little faith."

They took another look around at the deep-blue water of the lake, chopped white from a cool, brisk breeze.

"It's so beautiful," Josie said.

"Yeah, it's right up there with the view from home," Chef Claire said, nodding. Then she stared out at the water. "Do you think she's okay?"

"I do," Josie said, following Chef Claire's stare. "If she weren't, we wouldn't be here."

"No, we wouldn't. Let's call her after we get checked in."

"Absolutely," Josie said, nodding. "Okay, let's go do some cooking."

Chapter 2

Chef Claire came to a stop in front of La Bella Vita, a massive structure sitting amid spacious, landscaped grounds. They climbed out of the car and stretched as they looked around the hillsides surrounding the villa. Countless rows of fruitless, trellised vines dominated the view.

"It looks like they've finished the grape harvest," Chef Claire said.

"It's beautiful," Josie said, then glanced at a man and a woman who were grinning and waving as they approached. "I take it they're waving at you."

"They are," Chef Claire said, waving back.

"Chef Claire," a man in his fifties said as he brought her in close for a long embrace. "It's so good to see you."

"Hi, Marco," she said, returning his hug. "It's been way too long." She let go to embrace the woman. "How are you, Rosa?"

"Wonderful," she said, grimacing briefly from the hug. "You look fantastic."

"Thanks. You guys haven't aged a bit. I take it living here agrees with you."

"Haven't aged? You graduated years ago," Marco said, laughing. "There's no need to keep sucking up."

"Old habits die hard," Chef Claire said with a big grin. "Marco and Rosa Columbo, I'd like you to meet my directionally-challenged friend Josie."

They exchanged handshakes and pleasantries.

"Don't tell me you got lost coming in?" Rosa said.

"Yeah, a bit," Chef Claire said. "We somehow ended up heading north on the road running around the west side of the lake."

"It can be a tricky road," Marco said, nodding. "I still have trouble with it from time to time."

"See?" Josie said in mock protest.

"It certainly got my attention," Chef Claire said. "And we almost got run off the road by a very cranky guy in a Ferrari."

"A Ferrari?" Marco said, raising an eyebrow at his wife.

"Yeah, he was in a big hurry," Chef Claire said.

"What color was the car?" Rosa said.

"Bright yellow," Chef Claire said. "Why do you ask?"

"I'm not sure," Rosa said. "But I think you might have been dealing with Emerson Kingsley."

"Why does his name sound familiar?" Josie said.

"He's an industrialist from California," Marco said. "Big money, even bigger ego. And he was late for his tee time."

"Industrialist?" Josie said. "What does he do?"

"He manufactures various types of machinery and heavy equipment," Rosa said. "And if you believe the rumors, he dabbles on the dark side. You know, selling stuff to people who shouldn't have it."

"Lovely," Josie said with a frown.

"He's staying here at the villa?" Chef Claire said.

"Yes," Rosa said. "He and his wife are enrolled in the cooking school. It was her idea, but he agreed to come as long as he could play golf. There's a course on the western side of the lake he wanted to play today."

"Bronwyn," Rosa said, shaking her head. "Wait till you meet her."

"Don't start, dear," Marco said, mildly chastising his wife. "They're paying good money to be here."

"I know," Rosa said. "But I really don't like her."

"What's she like?" Chef Claire said.

"Beautiful, but entitled," Rosa said. "And she has an annoying habit of constantly taking selfies. As soon as she gets a look at you two, she's going to hate you. She won't like the competition."

"Aren't you sweet," Chef Claire said, laughing.

"Come on," Marco said. "Let's get you settled in. I'll have your bags brought up."

They strolled toward the front door.

"You have two restaurants now?" Rosa said.

"We do," Chef Claire said. "And both are doing well."

"No surprise there," Marco said, then glanced at Josie. "Chef Claire was the best student we ever had at the school. She was destined for greatness."

"Stop," Chef Claire said, taking another look around the grounds. "Speaking of doing great, it looks like you've got something very special here."

"Yes," Rosa said, squeezing her husband's arm. "We've been blessed."

Marco held the front door open then followed them inside. Chef Claire and Josie looked around the massive foyer and nodded.

"Wow," Josie whispered.

"It's amazing," Chef Claire said.

18

"Thanks," Marco said. "We like it. I'll give you a tour later. Follow me. I'll show you to your rooms."

They followed him up a long stairway leading to the second floor. Marco came to a stop at the top of the landing and pointed at a door off to his left.

"That will be your room, Chef Claire," Marco said. "Josie, you'll be right next door. The rooms adjoin, and if you like, you can open the inside door and turn it into a suite."

He motioned for them to follow him. He opened the door to Chef Claire's room and waved them in. Again, Josie and Chef Claire glanced around, stunned.

"It's incredible, Marco," Chef Claire said, then walked across the room and stepped out onto a large balcony. "And look at the view of the lake and mountains."

"We thought you'd like it," Rosa said.

"It's amazing," Chef Claire said, then glanced at Josie who was focused on a different view. "What is it?"

"Take a look," Josie said, nodding at a large pond near the villa.

"You gotta be kidding me," Chef Claire said, glancing at Marco. "Are they all yours?"

"The dogs?" he said, grinning. "They certainly are."

"Gorgeous," Josie said, continuing to stare out at them.

"I take it you're a dog person?" Rosa said.

"Yeah, you might say that."

"Josie's a vet," Chef Claire said. "And she and our friend Suzy run a Doggy Inn back at home."

"Interesting," Rosa said. "How many dogs do you have?"

"When we left a few days ago, we had seventy-six."

"We thought having four was a lot," Marco said, frowning. "My, that's a lot of dogs."

"Yeah, you'd think so, but not really. Would you mind if I went down and said hello to them?"

"Of course not," Rosa said.

"I have two Goldens," Chef Claire said. "But after looking at your guys, I might need to pick up a couple more."

"They're very happy here," Rosa said. "And, of course, we spoil them rotten."

"I'd be disappointed if you didn't," Chef Claire said, laughing. "So, what time does class start in the morning?"

"Nine," Marco said. "We're making pasta tomorrow. "Breakfast starts around seven-thirty. And dinner tonight is at eight. We'll be eating outside on the veranda. Weather permitting. Don't forget to bring your appetite."

"No problem there," Josie deadpanned. "I packed an extra one."

"What?" Rosa said.

"Nothing," Josie said. "Don't worry, I'll do my part."

"Okay, we'll get your bags up here, and you can get settled in," Rosa said. "Since you'll be playing with the dogs down at the pond, you might want to hold off on your shower."

"Got it," Chef Claire said.

"And there's a bowl of tennis balls sitting on the reception desk downstairs," Marco said. "You don't want to show up empty-handed."

"Thanks so much. It's so good to see you guys."

They both gave her another hug then waved to Josie and headed out.

"What a nice couple," Josie said, glancing outside at the four Goldens.

"They're the best," Chef Claire said. "I was surprised when I heard they were selling the culinary school and buying a villa in Italy."

"I think they made the right call. Okay, let's go get our dog fix."

Chapter 3

Josie did her best to duck but got caught in the crossfire. The onslaught came from three different directions, and the attack of the wet Goldens left her drenched and laughing. She knelt down and hugged all three tight. The other dog, a gorgeous male named Leo, sat in front of Chef Claire waiting for her to throw the tennis ball he had dropped at her feet. She fired the ball back into the large pond, and all four dogs tore off in hot pursuit then jumped into the water and swam toward the bobbing ball.

"The water has got to be cold," Chef Claire said, staring out at the dogs.

"It is," Josie said, wiping her sleeve across her forehead. "But they don't seem to mind."

"You think we could handle a couple more house dogs?" Chef Claire said, firing another tennis ball into the water.

"Uh, no," Josie said, laughing. "You about ready to head in and grab a shower?"

"Yeah, we should probably get going."

They started walking back to the villa and were soon caught by the dogs. Judging by the looks on their faces, they were wondering where the heck their playmates were going.

"We'll play again tomorrow," Chef Claire said, kneeling down to pet all four.

It was her turn to get drenched, and she patiently waited until the dogs finished shaking. She and Josie continued the walk. The dogs raced toward the back of the villa as soon as they spotted Rosa holding a gate open. She closed it behind them and spent the next few minutes doing her best to say hello without getting drenched. Eventually, she gave up and laughed and shrugged at Josie and Chef Claire.

They climbed the short set of steps leading to a veranda stretching the length of the front side of the villa and spotted a young man setting the table. He paused to give them and their wet look the once-over.

"It hasn't been raining, has it?" he said in English with a strong Italian accent.

"Chance of wet dog, one hundred percent," Josie said, extending her hand. "I'm Josie."

"Oh, you've been on pond duty. You've made four new friends for life. It's nice to meet you. I'm Enrico," he said, returning the handshake before turning to Chef Claire.

"I'm Chef Claire."

"Oh, the famous Chef Claire," he said, shaking hands with her. "Marco and Rosa are always talking about you. It's nice to finally meet you."

"Infamous is more like it," Chef Claire said. "How do you like working here?"

"It's wonderful. And Marco and Rosa are very good to me. I do a lot of different things around the place. Officially, they call me the caretaker."

"Well, mission accomplished," Josie said. "This place is amazing."

"Thanks," he said, counting the plates on the table. "Well, I need to finish setting up for dinner. It was nice meeting you. I'm sure we'll be seeing a lot of each other."

They smiled and waved and headed inside. As they walked up the stairs to the second floor, Josie again wiped a sleeve across her face.

"He seems happy."

"He does," Chef Claire said, nodding. "And why wouldn't he be?"

"Can't argue with that," she said, coming to a stop outside her door. "Is an hour enough time?"

"Plenty," Chef Claire said, reaching into her pocket for her key. "I'll knock on the inside door when I'm ready."

"Perfect," Josie said, inserting her room key.

They both paused when the door of the room next to Josie's opened. A man's head appeared, and he glanced to his left then flinched when he looked in the other direction and spotted them staring at him.

"Oh, hi," he said, his face reddening. "You caught me by surprise. Is it raining?"

"Only dogs," Josie deadpanned. "I think the cats must have the day off."

"Okay," he said, frowning. "I'm Georgio. I take it you're both here for the cooking school."

"We are," Chef Claire said.

"Good, good," he said, nodding. "I'm looking forward to it." He continued to nod his head as he searched for something to say. "Yes, it should be good," he said, still red-faced. "Well, I should go get ready for dinner."

He waved, glanced around as if he was unsure where to go, then headed down the stairs. They watched him go then frowned at each other.

"That was awkward," Chef Claire said.

"Indeed," Josie said. "Are you thinking the same thing I am?"

"If he just came out of his room, why would he go somewhere else to get ready for dinner?"

"That's the one. I have a funny feeling it isn't his room."

"And the way he looked up and down the hall before coming out was curious," Chef Claire said.

"To say the least. He didn't want to be seen leaving," Josie said, opening her door.

"Color me intrigued," Chef Claire said, heading into her room. "I'll see you in a bit."

Josie raised her glass of Prosecco and clinked glasses with Chef Claire.

"Well, here we are," Josie said. "Okay, let me see if I've got this right. A glass of something before dinner is called the aperitivo, right?"

"Very good," Chef Claire said, taking a small sip. "After this, we'll be having the antipasto course. I imagine it will be something like the ones we serve at C's."

27

"Works for me," Josie said, glancing around the room. "Should we go introduce ourselves?"

"It looks like they're all in mid-conversation, so let's hold off. I'm sure Marco and Rosa will introduce everyone as soon as we sit down for dinner," Chef Claire said.

"Excuse me for interrupting," an attractive woman somewhere in her forties said as she approached. "But aren't you, Chef Claire?"

"I am," Chef Claire said, frowning. "You look familiar, but I'm sorry. I don't remember your name."

"I'm Betty. Betty Smithsonian," the woman said, extending her hand. "Like the museum."

"I know we've met before," Chef Claire said. "This is Josie."

"Yes, I've seen you before, but only in passing," Betty said, beaming at Josie. "I live in Ottawa and have eaten at your restaurant in Clay Bay several times."

"Of course," Chef Claire said, nodding. "I remember. It's nice to see you, Betty."

"You drive down from Ottawa just to eat at the restaurant?" Josie said.

28

"At least once a month, weather permitting. It's so worth making the drive," Betty said, then looked at Chef Claire. "You're here for the cooking school?"

"We are," Chef Claire said.

"You're a guest lecturer?"

"No, just one of the students," Chef Claire said.

"That's odd," Betty said, frowning. "Do you really expect to learn anything new?"

"Of course. We can always learn, right? But I will also be doing some one on one work with Marco and Rosa outside of class. I'm trying to do a deep dive into some of the regional techniques."

"I see," Betty said. "My goal is to be a better cook at home. How about you Josie?"

"I'm afraid the only deep dive I'll be doing is into several bowls of pasta," she said, laughing. "But I would like to improve my skills in the kitchen. Chef Claire casts a long shadow."

"Don't sell yourself short. You're a great cook," Chef Claire said, then shook her head. "Pity I can't say the same thing about your ability to read a map."

"Funny," Josie said. "Are you here by yourself, Betty?"

"I am. None of my friends could make it, and I didn't want to wait until next year."

"What do you do?"

"I work for the Canadian government," she said, then shrugged it off. "It's pretty boring. Well, I'm so glad to see you. It should be a great week."

Marco and Rosa approached.

"I think we're ready to sit down for dinner," he said. "It's a bit chilly, but I think we'll be fine eating outside."

"Lead the way," Chef Claire said.

They followed him to the table, found their name cards and sat down. Chef Claire ended up sitting between Marco and Rosa. Josie was on Rosa's immediate right and Betty was on the other side of the table a few chairs down. Two servers approached the table each carrying a large tray. They set them down on opposite ends of the table and topped off everyone's glasses with Prosecco.

"Please help yourself," Marco said to the table. "It looks like we're missing one of our guests, but I'm sure she'll be along soon. So, let's get started. I'll handle introductions, but please feel free to jump in whenever you like."

He waited a few minutes until people had served themselves from the antipasto trays then continued.

"Rosa and I would like to welcome everyone. We'll be spending a lot of time together over the next week, so introductions are definitely in order. This is Chef Claire," Marco said. "She was a former student of ours back in the day when we ran the culinary school. She now has two restaurants, one in New York on the Canadian border, the other is in the Cayman Islands. And Rosa and I are delighted she's here."

A polite round of applause followed.

"Next to me is Chef Claire's friend Josie. She's a vet and her goal for the week is to improve her skills as a home cook."

"And eat," Josie said, eyeing her plate.

"A vet? Thank you for your service," said a heavily-jeweled, young woman from the other end of the table. "Which branch of the service were you in?"

"Canine corp," Josie said. "Actually, I'm a veterinarian."

"Oh, of course," the woman said, embarrassed. "Sorry."

"Don't worry about it," Josie said. "It was a logical assumption."

"That would be a first."

The bejeweled woman glared at the man sitting next to her then forced a smile and slid a piece of cheese into her mouth.

"Cheap shot," Josie whispered.

"It certainly was," Rosa said, nodding as she snuck a glance down the table.

"Okay," Marco said, sensing tension. "I'd like to introduce Emerson and Bronwyn Kingsley. That's a lovely necklace you're wearing, Bronwyn."

"Thank you, Marco," she said, slowly chewing her food.

"Emerson is a successful industrialist based out of California. Bronwyn tells us her major goal this week is to learn how to make pasta from scratch."

"It is," Bronwyn said, nodding. "I'd love to master it."

"Mixing eggs and flour?" Emerson Kingsley said with a laugh. "Gee, I don't know if I like your chances, dear. It sounds like a real challenge."

"What a jerk," Chef Claire whispered into her glass as she took a sip.

"Indeed," Rosa said, glancing over at her husband. "Move things along, Marco."

"Good idea," Marco said to his wife. He glanced around and his eyes settled on a couple sitting next to the now very cranky Bronwyn. "Next, I'd like to introduce Donato and Maria Peccati."

They both smiled shyly and gave everyone a small wave.

"The Peccati's run a catering company near Milan and are thinking about opening a restaurant," Marco said.

"We are," Donati said in halting English as he reached for his wife's hand. "Hopefully, sometime early next year."

"That is our goal," his wife Maria said, also struggling with her English.

"How exciting," Chef Claire said, raising her glass in salute. "Good luck."

"Thank you," the couple said in unison.

"Welcome," Marco said, then continued. "Sitting next to Emerson is Betty Smithsonian. Betty is from Canada and also hopes to improve her home cooking skills."

He raised his glass and everyone drank to her.

"Thank you," Betty said. "I'm very excited to be here."

"And we are glad to have you," Marco said, then focused on a young man with a long ponytail. "Next to Betty is Lance Jones. Lance is also from California and has dreams of becoming a professional chef."

"Actually, dream might be a bit of a stretch," he said, shrugging. "I'm here to see if I can get my parents off my back."

"I'm sorry?" Marco said, confused.

"I need to get a career going," he said. "If I don't, my folks are threatening to cut me off."

"I see," Marco said. "Becoming a chef wasn't your first choice?"

"Nah," the ponytailed man said. "Surfing was my first choice, but I blew my knee out a few years ago. After the surgery, I wasn't able to cut left the way I used to. It pretty much eliminated my chances of turning pro."

"I see," Marco said. "So, it was your second choice."

"Not really," Lance said. "I just sort of landed on cooking. I tried selling cars at my old man's dealership, washed out there, then he set me up in a couple of businesses that didn't make it. Then I did a year in college. Hated it and dropped out. After that, I bought some camera gear and traveled for a year with the idea of becoming a

34

photographer. When I got home, my parents took one look at my *portfolio* and gave me the ultimatum of getting what they consider a real job or lose my allowance."

"Allowance?" Josie said, frowning. "You still get an allowance?"

"Yeah, that's what my folks call it," Lance said. "Actually, it's more of a trust fund."

"Got it," Josie said.

"One night I was sitting around and hit on the idea of becoming a chef. It makes sense since I love to eat. I'm thinking about doing an Italian food truck. Food trucks are all the rage in California, but most of them serve Mexican food. I think a truck serving Italian food near the water will be a hit with the folks who hang out at the beach. And I figure I'll still have time to surf in the mornings. How hard can it be, huh?"

"Yes," Marco said, doing his best not to stare at him. "How hard can it be?" He glanced at Chef Claire. "You started with a food truck, didn't you, Chef Claire?"

"I did," she said, nodding.

"Cool," Lance said. "How was that?"

"Actually, it was a ton of work," she said.

"Bummer. But I can always hire somebody to do most of the work."

"You could," Chef Claire said. "But it's going to kill your profit margins."

"No problem," he said. "As long as it gets my parents off my back, I'll be fine." He nodded, pleased with his strategy and glanced around the table for affirmation.

Marco focused on a distinguished, overdressed man sitting across from Betty. "Finally, I'd like to introduce Georgio Russo."

Georgio beamed at everyone then raised his glass.

"Thank you, Marco," Georgio said. "I'm honored to be here."

"Georgio is an inventor," Marco said.

"Fascinating," Bronwyn said as she placed her elbows on the table and leaned forward.

"Not really," Georgio said, flashing her a smile. "But it's a living."

"It's more than a living, and you know it, Georgio," Emerson said, shaking his head. Then he glanced at his wife who continued to focus on the inventor. "You still find it fascinating what he does for a living?"

"I do," she said, barely glancing at her husband. "Taking an idea and creating something from scratch is amazing."

"What does he invent?" Chef Claire whispered to Rosa.

"As far as most people know, he invents gadgets people can use around the house," she said. "But if you believe the rumors, some of his other inventions are a bit more…deadly."

"I'm going to need a bit more," Chef Claire said.

"Weapon systems," Rosa whispered. "Spy gadgets, that sort of stuff. And he's not very discriminating about who he sells them to. Again, if you believe the rumors."

"What on earth is he doing at your cooking school?" Chef Claire said.

"He comes at least once a year," Rosa said. "Whenever he's looking for ideas for the next kitchen gadget, he'll spend the week at our school. He says this place inspires him. Over the years, he's become quite a good cook."

"We saw him earlier when we headed upstairs to shower," Josie said. "He was coming out of the room next to mine. But it's not his, is it?"

Rosa frowned and eventually gave Josie a quick shake of her head.

"Georgio's room is at the other end of the hall."

"Whose room is it?" Chef Claire whispered.

"The Kingsley's," Rosa said, dredging a piece of bread in olive oil.

"Interesting," Chef Claire said, spooning some marinated red peppers onto her plate.

"That explains the look on his face when he saw us," Josie said.

"What sort of look was it?" Rosa said.

"Like a kid who got caught with his hand in the cookie jar," Chef Claire said.

"What time did you see him?" Marco said, inserting himself into the conversation.

"It was around five-thirty," Josie said.

"I told you," Rosa whispered to her husband.

"They might have just been chatting," Marco said.

"I seriously doubt it, Marco," Rosa said with a snort. "What time did Emerson get back from playing golf?"

"It was after six," Marco said.

"You need to have a chat with Georgio," Rosa said, sneaking a glance down the table. "I don't want a repeat performance."

Josie and Chef Claire looked at each other, thoroughly confused.

"I'll talk to him after dinner," Marco said.

Rosa sat back in her chair, apparently mollified for the moment. Then she caught the look Josie and Chef Claire were giving her.

"I'll explain later," Rosa said. "How are the peppers?"

"Fantastic," Chef Claire said.

Everyone continued leisurely noshing from the antipasto platter and sipping Prosecco.

"I love eating like this," Chef Claire said, glancing out at the evening sky. "It's so relaxing."

"It is. Everyone is taking their time," Josie said.

"They are. It's the Italian way," Chef Claire said. "See, you're learning already."

"What I'm learning," Josie said, laughing as she reached for the bowl of red peppers. "Is that they better pick up the pace or get left in my dust."

Moments later, everyone at the table looked up when a woman strolled out onto the veranda. She waved to Marco and Rosa then sat down in the empty chair next to the inventor.

"I'm sorry I'm late," she said to no one in particular. "I took a nap and forgot to set my alarm."

Josie and Chef Claire stared at the women then at each other.

"No way," Josie said.

"I can't believe it," Chef Claire said.

"Do you know her?" Rosa said.

"We certainly do," Josie said. "She was the cause of the worst hangover I've ever had."

The woman began selecting items from one of the antipasto trays then spotted Josie and Chef Claire and sat back in her chair. Her confused stare eventually gave way to a frown almost resembling a small smile.

"Well, isn't this a small world?" she said.

"Hi, Natalie," Josie said.

"Nice to see you, Josie," Natalie said. "Hello, Chef Claire."

"How are you doing, Natalie?"

"I'm fine," she said, placing a napkin across her lap. "I can't believe it."

"You're here for cooking school?" Chef Claire said.

40

"I am," she said, scooping grilled squash onto her plate. "Let's catch up after dinner."

She began eating and was soon engrossed in a conversation with Georgio, the inventor.

"How do you know her?" Rosa said.

"We met her in Vegas," Chef Claire said. "Our friend, Suzy, was having her bachelorette party there and Natalie was working for the owner of the casino where we were staying."

"I see," Rosa said. "She seems quite severe."

"She is," Josie said.

"Is that a Russian accent?" Marco said.

"It is," Josie said. "And a word of advice, never drink vodka with her."

Chapter 4

While coffee and dessert were being served, Georgio Russo, the inventor and apparent afternoon acquaintance of Bronwyn Kingsley, got up and headed for Marco and Rosa. He came to a stop behind them, beamed at Chef Claire and Josie then spoke to Rosa.

"I couldn't help but notice you waving me over."

"Yes," Rosa said. "We definitely need to chat."

"I think I'll go say hello to Natalie," Chef Claire said, getting to her feet.

Josie followed suit, and they sat down next to the Russian woman. Georgio was already sitting between Marco and Rosa glancing back and forth at his hosts as they spoke to him in angry, hushed tones.

"I wonder what he did to offend them?" Natalie said, sitting back in her chair as a server removed her plate and placed dessert in front of her.

"Will you be having dessert and coffee here?" the server said to Josie and Chef Claire.

"Yes, please," Josie said, staring down at Natalie's dessert. "Chocolate cake?"

"I'm going to guess it's Torta Barozzi," Chef Claire said.

"Well done," the server said, nodding as he poured coffee for all three of them.

"What is it?" Josie said, beaming at the dessert in front of her.

"Chocolate cake," Chef Claire deadpanned.

"Funny," Josie said, digging in. She chewed slowly then her eyes went wide. "Oh, my goodness. It's unbelievable."

"It certainly is," Chef Claire said. "And rich. A little goes a long way, huh?"

"Speak for yourself," Josie said, then took a sip of coffee. "So, Natalie, at the risk of sounding rude, what the heck are you doing here?"

"Learning to cook, what else?" Natalie said, taking a bite of her dessert. "Delicious."

"Nah, I don't buy it," Josie said with a shake of her head. "You're working here, aren't you?"

"Working?" Natalie said, going for coy but not quite managing to pull it off. "What on earth would I be working on here?"

"Your spy stuff," Josie whispered as she leaned in close. "What else would I be talking about?"

"No, I assure you I'm merely here to learn. And eat and drink, of course."

"You decided to come to Italy and learn how to cook? By yourself?" Chef Claire said as she continued to work her way through her dessert.

"I did," Natalie said. "But I'm not here by myself."

"Really?" Josie looked around with a frown then glanced at the other end of the table. "You're here with the inventor?"

"I am," Natalie said. "Georgio asked me to come, and it sounded like a lot of fun. So here I am."

Josie, deep in thought, scratched her chin as she toyed with her dessert. Then she shrugged it off and took another bite.

"You're dating him?" Chef Claire said.

"I guess you could call it that," Natalie said without emotion.

"What's it like having two restaurants?"

Chef Claire looked across the table at the young Italian couple.

"It's a challenge," Chef Claire said. "But we have great people working for us. It makes all the difference. You're Maria, right?"

"Yes," she said, then placed a hand on her husband's arm. "And this is Donato."

"It's nice to meet you," Chef Claire said.

"Would you mind if we asked you some questions?" Maria said. "We have so many."

"Not at all," Chef Claire said, getting up and carrying her chair to the other side of the table.

Moments later, she was engrossed in conversation with the couple. Josie took another bite of her dessert before turning to Natalie.

"Can I ask you a question?"

"If you must," Natalie said.

"Are you and Georgio exclusive?"

"Interesting question," Natalie said, scowling at Josie. "And rather invasive. But, yes, I'd like to think so. Why do you ask?"

"Well, you know me, Natalie," Josie said, grinning. "Just being nosy."

45

"Yes, I remember," Natalie said, then a deep frown emerged. "And speaking of inquisitive people, I heard about what happened to Suzy's husband. Tragic. How is she doing?"

"She's going to make it," Josie whispered. "But it's been a tough couple of months."

"I'm sure it has," Natalie said, lighting a cigarette. "I like Suzy. She has a big brain and a big heart. An all-too-rare combination. Please send her my best wishes when you talk to her."

"I'll do that."

"I can't imagine what it's like to lose a loved one in that manner," Natalie said, glancing down the table at Georgio who was still in the middle of a tense conversation with Marco and Rosa.

"In your line of work, you must have seen it before, right?"

"Seen it, yes. Experienced it myself, no," she said, then exhaled audibly. "But we are here to relax and have fun. So, let's have no more talk of tragedy and loss."

"Works for me," Josie said, polishing off the last of her dessert. "Did you arrive today?"

"Yes, I got in late this afternoon," she said.

46

Georgio's chair made a racket when he pushed it back and got to his feet. Everyone at the table reacted to the noise and looked at him. He casually brushed imaginary lint off his sleeves then ran a hand through his salt and pepper hair.

"It was wonderful meeting all of you," he said, glancing around. "But I think I'm going to call it a night. Tomorrow's a school day."

Everyone chuckled and he stared down the table at Natalie and gave her a small nod.

"I'll see you all in the morning," he said as he headed inside the villa.

"If you'll excuse me," Natalie said, getting to her feet. "An early night sounds like a wonderful idea. Enjoy your evening."

Josie watched her go then caught a glimpse of the whispered conversation Natalie and Georgio were having in the doorway. Out of the corner of her eye, Josie caught Bronwyn closely watching the conversation the inventor and spy were having. When she made eye contact with Josie, she immediately glanced down and focused on her dessert.

"Is she okay?" Chef Claire said to Josie.

"Well, with Natalie, it's always hard to tell," she said, dredging her fork through the remnants on her dessert plate. "What is this sauce?"

"Fig and pomegranate," Chef Claire said.

"Interesting choice. Let me guess, they're in season at the moment."

"Well done," Chef Claire said, nodding. "I think fig season is over, but I imagine Marco and Rosa made some sort of preserves. And I like the way the pomegranate cuts the sweetness."

"Are you going to ask for the recipe?"

"First thing in the morning," Chef Claire said, laughing.

Marco got to his feet and looked around the table.

"It looks like everyone has finished eating," he said. "If you don't mind, Rosa and I would like to let the dogs out for a while."

"Geez, Marco, I don't know," Josie deadpanned. "That's asking a lot."

He laughed then addressed the table again.

"All we ask is you don't feed them," he said. "Especially any of the Torta Barozzi. Chocolate is a no-no for dogs."

48

Everyone nodded and made sure their plates were out of the way. Marco nodded at one of the servers. She opened a door, and all four Goldens trotted onto the veranda. They made a beeline for Marco and Rosa then began saying hello to the rest of the guests.

"They're beautiful," Bronwyn said, then reached down to pet one of the dogs. "Now, this is a dog, Emerson. Look at him."

"For the hundredth time, no," Emerson said, studying the dog without touching it. "We're not getting a dog."

"Maybe," she said dismissively as she rubbed the Golden's head. She pulled the dog close then snapped a picture of her and the dog. She set her phone on the table and looked at her husband. "Why don't you go to bed? You have an early tee time in the morning. I'll be up soon."

Emerson Kingsley was about to bark at his wife but remembered where he was. He gave her a dark glare then nodded before addressing the hosts.

"Thank you for a wonderful dinner," he said to Marco and Rosa. "And have a good time in class. I can't wait to see what you come up with for dinner tomorrow. Enjoy the rest of your evening."

He wheeled around and quickly departed.

"He's not coming to class?" Chef Claire said.

"No, he's only here for the golf. And the food and wine, of course," Bronwyn said.

"That's too bad," Chef Claire said.

"No," Bronwyn said, then finished the last of her coffee. "Not really."

Chapter 5

Marco glanced around the group ringing a massive kitchen island made of stainless steel but topped with a wooden work surface. He took a sip of coffee and waited until he had everyone's attention.

"Good morning," Marco said. "And welcome to day one of cooking school. Today we'll be making pasta. Since pasta plays a central role in Italian cuisine, we always start the week making pasta from scratch. And you'll be making fresh pasta a few more times during the week so don't worry if your first efforts aren't perfect. I'm not going to guarantee you'll be an expert by dinnertime, but I will promise you by the end of the week you'll be very proficient at turning flour and eggs into something truly magical."

Marco paused to take another sip of coffee. Then he pointed to the other side of the kitchen.

"Oh, I almost forgot," he said. "Help yourself to coffee and snacks. The cake is called Ciambella, a citrus sponge cake we often serve at breakfast. We'll be doing a day of

51

desserts later on in the week, and you'll get the recipe for the cake as well as several others." Marco laughed and glanced at Josie who was caught red-handed swallowing her final bite.

"What?" Josie deadpanned.

"From the look of things, it looks like some of you have already tried it."

"Well, it was just sitting there, and I figured it had to be for us, right?"

"Of course," Marco said, glancing at Chef Claire who continued to shake her head at the cake thief. "How is it?"

"Fantastic," Josie said.

"Help yourself," Marco said.

"Don't encourage her," Chef Claire said.

"Shut it."

"Okay," Marco said, grinning at Josie. "A healthy appetite. That's what we love to see around here." He addressed the group. "Generally, each day starts with a demonstration then you'll get a chance to try it out. After we turn you loose, Rosa and I will be coming around to help out if needed and make sure you're on the right track." He glanced around then smiled and clapped his hands once. "Okay, let's make some pasta."

Marco moved to the center of the island and made sure everyone could see him clearly.

"Don't worry about taking notes," he said. "Everything we'll be covering this week is outlined in the binders sitting on the table near the door. Remember to take one with you before you leave today." He sifted two cups of flour onto the work surface then pulled it into a pile.

"First, we need to talk a bit about flour. In Italy, there are three basic types of flour classified as either one, zero, or double-zero. The number designates the coarseness of the grind. Semolina flour is a coarse grind, all-purpose flour carries the zero designation, and double-zero is finely milled and produces a smooth-texture pasta. We could talk about flour all day, but you'd be bored to death. In your class materials, you'll find a section covering flour in detail. And for those of you so afflicted, it's a great cure for insomnia. For this demonstration, I'm using a 50/50 blend of semolina and all-purpose. But as you get comfortable making your own pasta, feel free to experiment."

Marco paused to look around and make sure there were no questions.

"Okay, let's continue. I like to sift my flour," Marco said. "Other people prefer not to. It's your choice. As soon

53

as you have the flour ready, make a well in the center. Next, crack two eggs into the well and add a pinch of salt."

He stood back and made sure everyone got a good look at what he'd created.

"There you have it," Marco said.

"That's it?" Emerson Kingsley said, frowning.

"I thought he was playing golf today," Josie whispered.

"I think he got rained out," Chef Claire said.

"Yes, Emerson," Marco said. "As far as the ingredients go. All we need to do is mix them together until we get a nice ball of pasta dough."

"I can't believe it," Emerson said, turning to his wife. "If that's all there is to it, why the heck am I paying thirty bucks for spaghetti and meatballs at Salvador?"

"You're paying for the ambiance, Emerson," Bronwyn said.

"Ambiance? Maybe if you cooked once in a while at home, we wouldn't have to worry about going out to find *ambiance*."

"That's why we're here, Emerson," Bronwyn said, her voice rising in pitch.

"Let's continue," Marco said. "A few things to remember. Always use fresh eggs at room temperature. And when it comes to kneading the dough, a rough surface like this wooden one works better than the marble or polished granite ones I'm sure several of you have at home. A rough surface helps the dough come together easier. If you don't already have one, you might want to pick up a large wooden cutting board to use."

Marco began working his fingers through the flour and egg mixture.

"This is definitely a hands-on process so don't be shy about working with the dough. I'm going to make the dough on top of the surface. I want to be sure everyone can see exactly what I'm doing. And since I've done this more times than I can remember, I'm not worried about making a mess. But if this your first time making pasta from scratch, I suggest you use a bowl during this stage. If you don't, there's a good chance you'll end up with flour and eggs all over the place. So, use a bowl until you feel comfortable working on the countertop. Trust me on this one."

Everyone laughed.

"Using your fingers, mix the eggs with the flour. Take your time to incorporate the eggs and flour a little at a time.

When everything is combined, you're ready to start kneading. And if you're using a bowl, take it out at this point and work on the counter. You're going to be kneading with your hands for about ten minutes. This is the most difficult part of the process, but it's essential to make sure you get the right consistency. If the dough is hard, there's probably too much flour. Add a splash of water, and it should solve the problem. If it's sticky and soft, add a bit of flour. The flour and the eggs must be fully incorporated and the only way to ensure it is by kneading. So, stay focused on your work. I'll be walking around to help you out if you need it."

"My mama uses a bit of oil when she makes pasta," Donato said in halting English.

"Thanks for mentioning that, Donato," Marco said. "If you're looking for more elasticity, you can add a splash of oil to the dough, but no more than a teaspoon for this recipe. And I should also point out the dough recipe we're working with today serves four."

"Not a chance," Josie whispered.

"Shhh. No talking in class," Chef Claire said.

They watched in silence for the next several minutes as Marco kneaded the dough. When he was happy with it, he passed it around.

"Try to get a feel for the dough. This is what you're looking for," Marco said, then waited until the ball of dough made its way back to him. "Now, we cover it with cling film and let the dough rest for about half an hour in a warm place. Or you can use a hand towel if you like."

"What about adding color or additional flavor to the pasta?" Betty Smithsonian said.

"We'll be doing that this afternoon, Betty," Marco said. "But to answer your question, if you're adding spices or herbs, or a vegetable like spinach, you do it during the kneading process." He smiled at her then addressed the group. "Okay, your turn. Pair off and use any of the workstations around the kitchen. If you have a question, just let me know."

"Which workstation do you want to use?" Chef Claire said.

"Let's grab the one closest to the cake," Josie said, pointing.

"Of course. What a dumb question," Chef Claire said, shaking her head as she followed Josie across the kitchen.

"Okay, two cups of flour, two eggs and a pinch of salt," Josie said, grabbing a measuring cup. "Sounds easy enough."

"Aren't you going to use a bowl?" Chef Claire said.

"No," Josie said. "Are you?"

"I've been making pasta for years," Chef Claire said as she began sifting flour onto the workstation. "But this is your first time."

"It is. But how hard can it be?"

Josie cracked two eggs into the well she had created in the flour and got to work. Chef Claire also began working but kept one eye on Josie who had already managed to knock down one side of the flour mound. Egg began streaming onto the workstation in different directions.

"Crap," Josie whispered.

"Problem?"

"Not at all. Just a little leakage. Nothing I can't handle."

Josie pulled the flour and egg back into more or less a pile and began working her fingers through it. Then she stopped and squinted before placing her hand over her mouth to stifle a sneeze.

"Geez," Josie said, reacting to the substance now covering her mouth and chin. "It wasn't the smartest thing I've ever done."

"You might want to start over," Chef Claire said, grabbing a dish towel and wiping the flour and egg off Josie's face.

"Good call," Josie said, taking the dish towel from Chef Claire.

They both glanced across the kitchen when they heard two voices getting louder. Emerson and Bronwyn Kingsley were in the middle of a heated conversation that didn't appear to be pasta related.

"Did you see what brought that on?" Josie said.

"I caught Bronwyn and Georgio exchanging a few haunting glances a minute ago," Chef Claire said. "It looks like Emerson did too."

"Do you think Natalie is the jealous type?" Josie said.

"I don't know. But given her background, I sure wouldn't be messing around with her boyfriend."

"The whole situation is weird," Josie said, depositing the remnants of her failed attempt in the trash. "And there's something strange about the inventor dude."

"Yeah, he kind of gives me the creeps," Chef Claire whispered. "You think he might be a spy like Natalie?"

"I suppose he could be," Josie said, building a fresh pile of flour on the workstation. "But he seems more like the kind of guy a spy like Natalie would be keeping an eye on."

"Now, there's an interesting theory," Chef Claire said as she began kneading her dough.

"Are you done incorporating already?" Josie said, reaching for an egg.

"I am. It's flour and two eggs," Chef Claire said. "It's not like we're making a five-course meal."

"Well, aren't you the teacher's pet," Josie deadpanned.

She was about to crack the egg when she sneezed loudly, scattering the pile of flour in several directions, one of which was all over her face and hair. Chef Claire took one look at her and burst into laughter. The rest of the group glanced over and broke into grins.

"Now I don't feel so bad," Betty Smithsonian said, her blouse covered in flour. "Are you okay?"

"Yeah, I'm fine," Josie said, again wiping her face with the dishtowel. She tossed the towel to one side then reached for the slice of Ciambella sitting on the workstation. She proceeded to drop the cake on the floor. Reaching down immediately, she snatched it off the floor and broke off a piece and popped it in her mouth.

"Are you out of your mind?" Chef Claire said.

"What?"

"You're going to eat it after it has been on the floor?"

"Three-second rule," Josie said, breaking off another piece and stuffing it into her mouth. "Besides, take a look around. This floor is clean enough to eat off."

"Which you've just proven," Chef Claire said, shaking her head as she went back to her kneading.

"You really get into your work, Josie," Marco said as he approached.

"Funny, Marco," she said, working her fingers through the mixture.

"Promise to be careful when we start working with knives," he said, laughing.

"I'm a whiz with knives, Marco. No worries there."

Chef Claire nodded in agreement.

"You should see her slice garlic with a scalpel."

Another outburst from the other side of the kitchen broke out. This time it was Emerson and Georgio who were exchanging words.

"Here we go," Marco said, shaking his head.

"You and Rosa were talking last night about how you didn't want a repeat performance out of Georgio," Chef Claire said.

"Yes, the last time he was here, he got…let's call it, close to one of the students," Marco said.

"I assume her husband didn't take it well?" Josie said.

"Fiancé," Marco said. "And no, he didn't take it well at all."

"Ouch," Chef Claire said. "What happened?"

"Georgio talked his way out of it," Marco said. "And then he left the villa early."

"Why do you let him keep coming back?" Chef Claire said.

Marco took a deep breath and exhaled audibly.

"Because he's an investor in the place," Marco said. "And we also get a cut of every kitchen gadget he comes up with. But his womanizing can be a problem."

Emerson Kingsley tossed an impressive string of expletives at his wife, and the inventor then stormed out of the kitchen. The rest of the group, embarrassed by the scene, focused on their work and kneaded like there was no tomorrow.

"I think I've finally got it," Josie said, holding up her ball of dough.

Marco accepted the dough from her, gently pressed it with his fingers and nodded.

"Very good," Marco said with a grin. "It's a lot easier when the dough stays on the table and out of your hair."

"You didn't tell me he was a comedian, Chef Claire," Josie said, making a face at Marco.

"You'll get used to me," he said. "Okay, wrap your dough and let it rest." He turned to address the group. "We'll take our morning break now. Please be back in a half-hour, and we'll roll the dough. And this afternoon, I'll show you three simple sauces. Then you'll each be making a dish you want to serve at dinner tonight."

The class began filing out as Chef Claire topped off her coffee.

"Can we do the interview now, Marco?"

"Oh, right," he said, nodding. "For your food blog. Sure. We can use my office."

"Are your dogs around?" Josie said.

"They're probably in the living room," Marco said. "They like to hang out by the fireplace when it's raining."

"I'll see you in a bit," Josie said, giving them a finger wave as she left the kitchen.

Chapter 6

As promised, Josie found all four Goldens in the living room, and they hopped to their feet as soon as she entered. She sat down on the floor, and they draped themselves over her. Josie glanced up when she heard the sound of someone walking into the room.

"Oh, hi, Bronwyn."

"You certainly love dogs, don't you?" she said, sitting down on one of the couches.

"Yeah, guilty as charged," Josie said, climbing to her feet and sitting down across from her. "Are you okay?"

"I'll be fine," she said, shrugging. "I knew it was a mistake to bring Emerson along on the trip.

One of the Goldens trotted over to Bronwyn, and she tentatively petted the dog's head.

"I'm not much of a dog person," she said. "But these are very gentle."

"They're one of my favorite breeds," Josie said. "But I love them all."

"You must have dogs at home."

"We do. Seventy-six at last count."

"I beg your pardon?" Bronwyn said, raising an eyebrow.

"We run an inn for dogs," Josie said. "You know, veterinary services, groom and board, obedience classes, a big rescue program. If it's dog-related, we pretty much do it. Did Emerson leave?"

"The rain has stopped so he's going golfing."

"It's none of my business, but he seemed upset."

"He's convinced Georgio and I are still an item," she said, flinching briefly when one of the Goldens hopped up on the couch and dropped its head in her lap. "Well, aren't you friendly?"

Josie gave her a blank stare. Eventually, Bronwyn continued.

"I used to date, Georgio," she said with a shrug.

"And you came here with your husband knowing your ex-boyfriend was going to be here?"

"I didn't know Georgio was going to be here," she said, stroking the dog's head. "Are all Golden Retrievers like this?"

"Pretty much," Josie said. "And Golden puppies will make your heart melt."

Bronwyn nodded as if considering getting one.

"I told Georgio we were coming here," she said. "But I had no idea he'd show up."

"Marco said he's one of his investors," Josie said.

"He is. And Emerson is thinking about throwing some money in. From what I hear, the winery is struggling."

"Complicated situation."

"It can be," she said. "I actually met Emerson during the time I was dating Georgio. He was doing some work with Emerson's company, and we went to a party at his house one night. When I met Emerson, things took off from there."

"You dumped Georgio for Emerson?" Josie said, treading carefully.

"Pretty much. Georgio had already proven himself incapable of being faithful, so I knew there wasn't much of a future with him. And Emerson was different back then."

"But still very rich, right?" Josie said.

"Scary rich," Bronwyn said, nodding. "And that played a big part. But it wasn't all of it." She shook her head and glanced at Josie. "It sounded like I was trying to convince myself, not you, didn't it?"

"Maybe a little," Josie said, making room for another of the Goldens on the couch. "How did Georgio take it when you ended the relationship?"

"One thing I've learned about Georgio over the years is the way to get his undivided attention is by telling him he can't have something."

"I know people like that," Josie said, nodding. "And as soon as they get what they want, they lose interest."

"Exactly," Bronwyn said. "I couldn't believe it when he showed up with the Russian woman. What a weirdo she is."

"Natalie's okay," Josie said. "We met her in Vegas a few months ago. She just takes some getting used to."

"I have no intention of getting used to her," she said. "Do you know what she does for work?"

"Actually, I do," Josie said, frowning. "But I'm not sure I should talk about it."

"Ooh, I smell a secret," Bronwyn said. "Well, with her personality, I know she's not a hooker."

"No, she's not," Josie said, laughing. "Let's say she spent several years working for the government and leave it there."

"I can't understand why he's interested in her. She's so not his type."

"I should probably tell you we saw Georgio coming out of your room yesterday," Josie said softly.

"He told me," she said, nodding. "I was taking a nap while Emerson was playing golf and Georgio knocked on my door. We talked and reminisced for a while, and I *almost* slipped up. I finally told him he needed to leave. He wasn't happy about it."

"But your husband doesn't believe nothing happened?"

"No, he doesn't," Bronwyn said, glancing down at the Golden sprawled across her lap. "This guy is insatiable."

"They do love attention," Josie said, laughing. "How did Georgio end up working with your husband?"

"He invented something he wanted my husband's company to manufacture," Bronwyn said.

"Some sort of kitchen gadget?"

"No. The kitchen inventions are just a hobby for Georgio. Or maybe cover would be a better term for it," she said. "And it gives him a good excuse to visit the villa."

"What was it?"

"It was a gun," she said with a shrug. "A big gun."

"Really?"

"I thought you must have heard by now how Georgio makes most of his money," Bronwyn said.

"I heard he invented stuff you could use around the house."

"Sometimes. Actually, most of what he invents are things you can use on the battlefield."

"He's an arms dealer?"

"Sort of," she said with a frown. "Basically, he travels the world meeting with various thugs and third-world leaders looking for new and interesting ways to keep their rivals under control. Georgio figures out what they need then heads off to make it. When he has a working prototype ready to go, he starts talking to people like my husband to see if they can mass produce it for the price he's willing to pay."

"Is that even legal?" Josie said.

"I seriously doubt it. But as long as they don't get caught," she said with a shrug.

"I guess that's one way to look at it," Josie said. "He invents weapons. Geez, what a weird way to make a living."

"Guns, electronics, satellite components, you name it. Rumor has it he's developing some computer malware a lot of people can't wait to get their hands on."

"He sounds like a genius."

"He is. A total psycho with a host of other delightful quirks but definitely a genius," Bronwyn said as she snapped a selfie of her and the Golden draped across her lap. She glanced at the photo and frowned. "My hair's a mess."

Chef Claire entered the living room, and all four dogs trotted over to greet her. She sat down on the floor and was soon flat on her back and buried beneath fur and wagging tails. Laughing, she made her way back into an upright position.

"Marco wants us back soon," she said. "But I had to say hi to these guys."

Georgio and Betty Smithsonian entered but paused in the doorway.

"I'm sorry to interrupt," Georgio said. "But Marco is ready to start class."

"We're on our way," Chef Claire said, getting to her feet.

Georgio and Betty headed toward the kitchen and Bronwyn glanced at Josie.

"I was wondering how long it was going to take him to set his sights on her," she said, shaking her head.

"Betty?" Josie said.

"Yeah."

"Are you sure?"

"Just watch," Bronwyn said, then exited the living room. She called out over her shoulder as she headed down the hallway. "I know him better than he knows himself. I'm surprised he hasn't made a play for you two."

Chef Claire followed Josie out of the room and leaned in close.

"What's she talking about?" Chef Claire whispered.

"Georgio's inability to stop chasing women," Josie said.

"Betty?"

"According to Bronwyn, she's next up on his list."

"She is pretty. Do you think Natalie knows?" Chef Claire said. "They are here together."

"I'm beginning to think Natalie might be here for another reason," Josie said.

"Like what?"

"I think she might be working here."

"Spy stuff?"

"I think it's a possibility," Josie said, then shook her head. "The heck with it. We're on vacation. Forget it. Did you finish your interview?"

"Almost. We'll do the last bit after class."

"Okay," Josie said. "Let's go roll some dough."

"Try not to get it all over you," Chef Claire deadpanned.

"Yeah, I'll do my best," Josie said, punching her gently on the shoulder. "All of a sudden, I've got a bad feeling."

"Serves you right for eating cake off the floor."

Chapter 7

Marco sipped coffee while waiting for everyone to return. He motioned for the group to assemble around the main island where a large, stainless-steel object was sitting next to a large rolling pin.

"Welcome back," he said, setting his coffee down and picking up the rolling pin. "It's time for us to roll out our pasta dough. I imagine you're all expecting to be taught the easiest way to use a rolling pin to get your dough to the right thickness and just the way you want it. So, here's the best way to use it."

Marco raised his arm and tossed the rolling pin into a large trash bin. The class laughed long and hard.

"I know we're constantly talking about preserving Italian culinary traditions, but when it comes to archaic techniques, some things are better left to the past." He placed a hand on top of the stainless-steel device. "And trust me, if our mothers and grandmas had even gotten their hands on this baby, they would have also tossed their rolling pin in the trash. You're looking at the GRM. It's an acronym for Georgio, Rosa, and Marco, and it's the latest and greatest. It is without a doubt the best pasta maker on the planet."

"Well, thank you, Marco," Georgio said, beaming. "But you deserve a lot of credit as well. You and Rosa made a big contribution."

"Only with some ideas about what it should do," Marco said, shaking his head. "You made it happen. And it's beautiful."

"Grazie."

"The GRM isn't even on the market yet, but when it is, I have no doubt it will win all sorts of product-of-the-year awards. And the best news for you is Georgio has kindly donated one to every student here this week."

Murmurs of appreciation and a round of applause broke out. Georgio continued to beam as he waited it out.

"You're very welcome," Georgio said. "All I ask is you enjoy it and tell your friends where they can get their own. Major retailers everywhere, Amazon, all the usual suspects."

He waited out the laughter.

"Since you're here, Georgio, why don't you do the honors of showing everyone how to use it?"

"I'd be happy to do that," he said, moving around the island until he was directly behind the GRM. "When we first started talking about developing a new pasta maker, we decided it should do everything, be durable, and very easy to clean. And I think you'll soon see we accomplished all three objectives. Basically, there are two types of pasta makers. There's a roller kind that flattens the dough and cuts it into things like spaghetti and linguine. The second type does extrusion and pushes the dough out. By attaching one of the various dies that come with the GRM, you can make every type of pasta shape, including hollow tubes you can stuff with the filling of your choice. Instead of either or, we decided the GRM had to both roll and extrude."

"It's beautiful," Chef Claire said, giving the machine a loving stare.

"A lot of women only drool like that over jewelry or shoes," Josie deadpanned. "Your knees go wobbly over kitchen appliances."

"Shut it."

"In the back of the machine is a well where you can add your ingredients," Georgio said. "I still prefer to use my hands when I'm making the dough, but many people like the convenience of having the machine do it for them.

76

And the GRM has a motor, so the days of having to turn a crank are long gone."

"Rosa and I have been using it for a couple of months, and we simply love it," Marco said. "Is there anything else you need to tell them, Georgio, or should we turn them loose?"

"I've always found the quickest way to learn is by jumping right in," Georgio said.

"Good," Marco said. "Okay, folks, for the next couple of hours, you'll be making the pasta of your choice. And we've got lots of pre-made dough in the fridge so don't worry about running out. After lunch, Rosa and I are going to cover three simple sauces. And your assignment will be to pair the pasta of your choice with one of the three sauces we cover in class. We'll be sampling all your dishes at dinner tonight."

The group nodded and murmured to each other.

"Yes, exciting stuff," Marco said with a grin. "Take your time deciding which of the three sauces will work best with the pasta you end up using. And just so you know, Rosa and I will be showing you a basic marinara, a simple pesto, and an olive oil and butter sauce. We'll also be covering some additional ingredients you can add to all three to make them extra special. But remember the cardinal rule. It's not the *quantity* of ingredients you use, it's the *quality* of the ingredients prepared well that is the secret to great Italian cooking." Marco paused to glance around at everyone. "I know it sounds like we're throwing a lot at you on your first day, but I'm sure you'll all be able to handle it. So, have fun with your new kitchen toy. Georgio and I will be happy to help you out if you have questions or aren't clear how the GRM works." Marco started to walk away but stopped. "Oh, one more thing. Since Emerson isn't here, why don't you work in groups of three? It will give you a chance to get to know some of the other folks in class a bit better."

"How cool is this?" Chef Claire said, heading for the workstation.

"Try to control yourself," Josie said, laughing. "C'mon, Natalie. Join us."

"What a good idea," Natalie said, carrying her GRM to the workstation. "It'll be like cheating on a test from the smartest kid in the room."

"Aren't you sweet," Chef Claire said.

"Something I don't often hear," Natalie said with a puzzled frown.

Musings While I Wander

Italy in October – 2

We just finished our first day of class where we learned to make fresh pasta. And I'll be doing a post soon about the science and art behind the process of turning a few basic ingredients into a dough used to create dozens of different kinds of pasta that will have your family and friends raving. But for this post, I wanted to do an interview with Marco Columbo, my mentor from culinary school and one of the owners of La Bella Vita, the magnificent villa Josie and I are staying at. Marco and his wife, Rosa, sold the culinary school they ran in California then bought the villa and moved to Northern Italy. The school, an intense, one-week program where students are immersed in the techniques of Italian cooking, is conducted on-site and classes are led by Marco and Rosa.

He has kindly agreed to an interview, and I'm hoping with a little encouragement he'll be willing to share the recipe for Torta Barozzi, an incredible dessert we enjoyed last night. So, let's get started.

Chef Claire – Thanks for agreeing to chat, Marco. What's so funny?

Marco – I'm just watching Josie trying to get flour and dough out of her hair. Does she always make a mess when she's cooking?

Chef Claire – She does. But be sure to watch when she slices garlic with a scalpel. She's a magician.

Marco – I'll remember that. (calling out) Josie, I suggest you use a towel and a brush on your hair before you take a shower. Unless you're trying to invent pasta dough shampoo.

Chef Claire – What did she say?

Marco – I'm not comfortable using that sort of language. Okay, Chef Claire, let's chat. And since you've been sucking up in class all day, I suppose you want my recipe for Torta Barozzi?

Chef Claire – Of course. Anything that good should be shared with the world. Isn't that what you always used to tell your students?

Marco – Touché. You always did pay attention in class. Of course, I'll share it. Anything for you, Chef Claire.

Chef Claire – Thank you, Marco. Let's start with some history. Where did Torta Barozzi come from?

Marco – It was created in the late 19th century by a pastry chef by the name of Eugenio Gollini who lived in Vignola, a small town a couple of hours south of here. According to legend, he spent a long time pursuing his goal of creating a new cake. And he continued working on it until he was finally satisfied with the result.

Chef Claire – I'm glad he persevered. But why isn't it called Torta Gollino?

Marco – He originally named it torta nera which translates into 'black cake' but it was renamed Torta Barozzi in honor of Jacopo Barozzi. He was a famous 16th-century architect from Vignola who once did work for the Pope.

Chef Claire – I heard the original recipe is still considered a state secret by the descendants of the guy who invented it.

Marco – It is. And the debate rages on about what should and shouldn't be in the cake. But like many other recipes, I played around with it until I hit on one I enjoy the most.

Chef Claire – We'll eat while others argue, right?

Marco – Indeed. Anyway, I like my recipe. As do my family and friends. Should we begin?

Chef Claire – Absolutely. Let's begin with the ingredients.

Marco – There are dozens of variations to the recipe and all of them delicious. So, you really can't go wrong. Some recipes include ground coffee and rum. And it's rumored the original recipe calls for peanuts. I prefer almonds, but I had one recently with hazelnuts and it was delicious. I used to include the coffee but eventually eliminated it from my recipe. And as soon as I decided to use almonds, I swapped out the rum for Amaretto, which as you know is an almond-flavored liqueur.

Chef Claire – What's in your version?

Marco – Dark chocolate, butter, eggs, sugar, and almonds. And I use a splash of Amaretto to really bring out the flavor of the almonds.

Chef Claire – That's it?

Marco – It is. You know the Italian philosophy.

Chef Claire – Only include ingredients that absolutely have to be there?

Marco – Exactly. I assume you'll be including the recipe with detailed instructions later on.

82

Chef Claire – I will.

Marco – Then I won't bother going through all the steps. But I will share a few tips. First, be sure to toast the almonds very slowly. I like to use a dry pan, but the oven is fine. Either way, use very low heat and wait until they toast all the way through to the middle. By the time they're done, your kitchen will smell fantastic.

Chef Claire – Easy one. What else?

Marco – Grind the almonds and the sugar well. I use a coffee grinder, but a blender also works. Since it's a flourless cake, the mixture of ground almonds and sugar, the almond-flour if you will, is the only dry ingredient in the cake. The rest of the recipe is straightforward, and I'm sure your instructions will walk people through the process. As you saw last night, I finish the dish with a sprinkle of powdered sugar after the cake squares are cut and ready to be served.

Chef Claire – How many different sauces and compotes do you serve with the cake?

Marco – I have a lot of different ones. It depends on what is in season. I use macerated berries or tart cherries and often include another splash of Amaretto to carry the almond flavor through the dish. But other people like a dollop of whipped cream while others prefer to just let the cake speak for itself. The one we had last night was a fig jam and pomegranate sauce cooked down until it's *almost* a glaze. Not exactly traditional, but people seem to like it. The only other advice I have is to take your time and have some fun with it. Don't be afraid to experiment. Since the original recipe is under lock and key, who's gonna argue authenticity with you?

Chef Claire – A rebel to the end, huh? What about storage? Since Josie won't always be around, I assume you'll have leftovers.

Marco – Keep it wrapped in the foil and out of the refrigerator. It will last for up to a month, perhaps even a bit longer.

Chef Claire – Not around our house it won't. Thanks so much, Marco.

Marco – Happy to do it. And here's a little extra bonus recipe for you.

Chef Claire – I can't believe it. Your recipe for Il Pane dei Morti?

Marco – The very one. Bread of the dead. I only make them a few times a year. And All Souls' Day is one of those times.

Chef Claire – I remember the cookies from when you made them for us at culinary school. I couldn't believe how good they were. Moist and chewy. Rich and dense. They're incredible. Thanks so much, Marco. I'll make good use of both these recipes.

Marco – Happy to do it, Chef Claire. But I should get back to the kitchen before class resumes. Big day tomorrow. All Saint's Day. And I have to go through the menu with Rosa and the rest of the staff.

Chef Claire – That's right. I forgot tomorrow is a national holiday.

Marco – It is. A day of feast. And all of you will be helping out with the preparations.

Chef Claire – You're such a slave driver.

Marco – You wouldn't have it any other way. Oh, I almost forgot. It's going to be cold this evening, so we'll be eating inside. After dinner, we'll head out to the veranda to watch the fireworks over the lake. It's Halloween.

Chef Claire – Halloween is celebrated in Italy?

Marco – It is. Technically, it's All Saints' Eve, but costume parties and such continue to grow in popularity. And we do love our fireworks.

Chef Claire – Thanks for taking the time to talk with me, Marco. And thanks so much for the recipes.

Torta Barozzi

Ingredients

- 4.5 ounces toasted and ground almonds
- 9 ounces dark chocolate
- 4.5 ounces butter
- 4 eggs
- 6 ounces sugar
- 1 tablespoon Amaretto

Instructions

- Preheat oven to 350F/ 180C
- Toast the almonds on the stove or in the oven using very low heat. When completely toasted,

grind almonds and half the sugar in a grinder or blender.

- Melt the butter and chocolate in a bowl over a simmering pot of water. Set aside to cool until lukewarm.

- Separate the eggs, reserving the whites.

- Beat the yolks with the remaining sugar until the sugar has dissolved and the mixture is thick and creamy.

- Add the toasted almond "flour" first, then incorporate the egg mixture, melted butter and chocolate, and Amaretto.

- Beat the egg whites until stiff and gently fold into the mixture. The consistency of the cake batter should be thick but still pourable.

- Pour the mixture into a 12-inch, non-stick springform pan. (Or cover bottom and sides of pan with parchment.) It should only be the width of a couple of fingers.

- Bake for 25-30 minutes. Test for doneness with a toothpick. Torta Barozzi should have a thin, dry crust with a moist center. (A bit 'gooey' is just fine.)

- Gently remove from pan and let cool before cutting. If you're not eating it right away, wrap the cake in foil.

- To serve, cut into small squares and top with powdered sugar, a dollop of whipped cream, or fresh berries of your choice. (Cut the cake carefully using a serrated knife. It can be a bit fragile.)

Pane Dei Morti (Bread of the Dead)

Ingredients

- 6 ounces amaretti biscuits (1)
- 12 ounces ladyfinger biscuits (1)
- 1 cup almonds (2)
- 1 cup pine nuts (2)
- ½ cup dried figs
- ½ cup raisins
- 2 cups all-purpose flour
- 6 large egg whites
- 1 ½ cups sugar
- ½ cup cocoa powder

- ½ cup Vin Santo or another sweet dessert wine
- 1 tsp. baking powder
- 1 tsp. ground cinnamon
- ¼ tsp. ground nutmeg
- Pinch of salt
- Powdered sugar, for dusting

1. Amount of each biscuit can be modified to taste as long as the total weight isn't exceeded.
2. Amount of nuts can be adjusted down slightly according to taste.

Over time, you'll figure out your preferred balance.

Instructions

- Preheat the oven to 350 F. Line baking sheets with parchment paper and set aside.
- In a food processor, grind the amaretti biscuits, the ladyfinger biscuits, and the almonds

into a flour. Add the figs and process until a clumpy dough forms.

- In a large mixing bowl, combine the biscuit, almond and fig dough with the raisins, flour, sugar, cocoa powder, baking powder, cinnamon, nutmeg, salt and whole pine nuts. Using your hands, work the ingredients together until completely incorporated.

- Add the egg whites and dessert wine to the bowl and mix well.

- Shape the cookies: scoop out a golf ball-sized portion of dough and shape each one into a flat, oval biscuit. Place the biscuits on the prepared baking sheet, leaving space between them.

- Bake for 30-35 minutes or until slightly puffed and crisp. Cookies should be a darkish brown color and set. Lift one up carefully with a spatula and check to make sure the bottom side is cooked.

- Place cookies on a cooling rack and allow to cool before sifting the icing sugar on top.

Chapter 8

Josie cast a loving stare at the collection of dishes then spotted the one she was looking for. She helped herself to a generous portion then settled back into her seat. She was about to take her first bite when she caught the look Chef Claire was giving her.

"What?" Josie said, raising an eyebrow at her.

"Nothing."

"I wouldn't be a very good classmate if I didn't try everyone's dish," Josie said.

"I see. So, you're taking one for the team?"

"Exactly," Josie said, then slid a forkful of penne tossed in a pesto sauce into her mouth. "This is fantastic."

"Thank you," Betty Smithsonian said from the other side of the table. "I was worried I used too much garlic."

"It's perfect," Josie said, stabbing more of the dish with her fork.

"As soon as you've all finished eating, we'll head out to the veranda. It seems to have warmed up a bit, and the view of the fireworks is much better out there," Marco said, then raised his glass in toast. "I'd like to salute all of you. You did a great job on your dishes."

Everyone clinked glasses and sat back in their chairs, full but content. Gradually, people began filing out of the dining room onto the veranda. Josie polished off the last of her penne and exhaled as she pushed the plate away.

"Did you save room for dessert?" Chef Claire said.

"Rhetorical, right?" Josie said, then glanced down the table where Marco and Rosa were sitting. "Can we help you clean up?"

"No, thanks, Josie," Rosa said. "While we want everyone to feel at home, you are all still guests. Enrico and the rest of the staff will take care of it."

"Okay," Josie said, getting up from the table. "Are you ready, Chef Claire? Limoncello and dessert await."

"You're unbelievable," Chef Claire said, shaking her head as she stood up. "Thanks again, guys. It was a great meal."

"It was a lot of pasta," Marco said, laughing as he gestured for everyone to head outside.

"Are you coming, Bronwyn?" Chef Claire said to the woman sitting next to her.

"I'll be out in a minute," she said, toying with the remnants on her plate.

Josie and Chef Claire headed for the outside doors. Josie glanced over her shoulder at Bronwyn who continued to sit quietly staring off into the distance.

"Is she okay?" Josie whispered.

"She and Emerson had a huge fight right before dinner," Chef Claire whispered back. "He told her he wants to take a little break."

"A break from her?"

"Yeah," Chef Claire said. "Emerson is convinced there's still something going on between her and Georgio."

"What do you think?"

Chef Claire shrugged then stretched out in a lounge chair.

"Anything is possible," she said. "I think all three of them have some sort of weird love-hate thing going."

"Something about this group is bugging me," Josie said, stretching out in the lounger next to Chef Claire.

"How so?" Chef Claire said, glancing over.

"Well, there's the connection between Georgio and Emerson. If Georgio invents weapons and crap like that, it probably means Emerson's company is manufacturing some of them."

"I was thinking the same thing," Chef Claire said. "I thought the FBI and CIA were all over black market weapons."

"I'm sure they are," Josie said. "Unless they're working with our government."

"You mean, selling stuff to people who are currently on our side?"

"Yeah. You know how all that works."

"Thankfully, I don't," Chef Claire said. "But I understand the basics. Today's best buddy is tomorrow's terrorist."

"Exactly. And what the heck is Natalie doing here?" Josie said. "She's supposed to be retired."

"Yeah, I know," Chef Claire said. "But I never bought that story. It was pretty clear from our time in Vegas she was still involved in all sorts of stuff. And I sure don't buy the idea she and Georgio are a couple."

"It's probably just a casual thing," Josie said.

"Like us, I don't think Natalie does casual," Chef Claire said, shaking her head. "And I seriously doubt if she's here just to learn how to make pasta."

"I did like the dish she made," Josie said.

"You liked them all."

"Didn't you?"

"Yeah, the ones I had were good. But I didn't try the surfer dude's dish. I saw the look on Betty's face when she tasted it," Chef Claire said, nodding.

"It was edible. Barely."

"Natalie is up to something."

"I'm getting a weird vibe from a couple of other people," Josie said.

"Which ones?" Chef Claire whispered, glancing around as she sat up on the lounge chair.

"Well, for one, the surfer dude," Josie said. "Something about him really bugs me. He's always hovering."

"Yeah, I noticed."

"And there's something about Betty that bothers me," Josie said.

"What's wrong with her?"

"She's compulsively sweet and nice," Josie said.

"She's Canadian. What else would you expect?"

"No, I get all that," Josie said, shaking her head. "But her niceness is disarming. And she's always following up with questions."

"She is in cooking school," Chef Claire said. "She's supposed to ask a lot of questions."

"No, I heard her talking with Georgio over dinner. And while she was positively sweet the whole time, she was definitely pumping him for information."

"Well, Bronwyn did say that Georgio was definitely going to try to get his hooks into her," Chef Claire said. "Maybe it's working."

"Maybe. But I think something's lurking below the surface."

"Lurking?" Chef Claire said, laughing.

"Yeah, lurking is the word for it."

"You've been listening to Suzy too much," Chef Claire said. "Which reminds me, we need to give her a call tonight."

They both sat up when they heard a woman scream. Everyone on the veranda raced inside and found Rosa in the dining room standing over Bronwyn who was laying on the tile with a smile frozen on her face. The top three buttons of her blouse were undone, and her lips, freshly painted with bright-red lipstick, were puckered.

"Bronwyn," Emerson said, kneeling down to get a close look at his wife.

"What the heck?" Chef Claire said.

"This is not good," Josie whispered as she stared down at the lifeless woman.

"Let me take a look," Natalie said, shouldering her way through the group. She knelt down, pressed her fingers against Bronwyn's neck then shook her head. "I'm sorry. But she's gone."

"No," Emerson whispered. "It's not possible."

He started to reach for his wife, but Natalie stopped him by gently placing a hand on his arm.

"Don't touch her," Natalie said.

"What?" Emerson said, glaring at the Russian woman.

"She's right," Betty said. "The paramedics need to take a look before you move her. And maybe the police."

"What the heck happened?" Marco said to Rosa.

"I have no idea," she said, tears streaming down her cheeks. "I was heading outside to watch the fireworks, and I just happened to see her out of the corner of my eye."

"We need to call the police," Marco said, patting his pockets in search of his phone.

"I'll make the call," Georgio said. Obviously shaken, he grabbed his phone off the table and punched in a number. "I need to report a death. Yes, I'll hold."

"Or maybe more than just a death," Josie whispered to Chef Claire.

"You're thinking murder?" Chef Claire whispered back.

"Aren't you?"

"I was trying not to think about it."

"Good luck with that," Josie said, taking a final look at the woman sprawled out on the floor.

Chapter 9

Commissario Bruno was a tall, rumpled man somewhere in his thirties who seemingly had perpetual fatigue etched on his face. It was the look of someone who either spent way too much time working or had a newborn baby at home. Judging by the deep, dark circles around his eyes, perhaps it was both. But it was his companion that captured Josie's attention. She shrieked when she first noticed him and bent down to welcome the visitor. The dog returned the greeting and wagged his tail.

"You've got a Newfie," Josie said, hugging the dog.

"Si," he said, nodding as he studied the look of joy on Josie's face.

"He's gorgeous," she said, getting to her feet but continuing to rub the dog's head. "I have one as well."

"Il suo nome è Rico," the detective said.

"How's your Italian, Marco?" Josie said with a frown as she looked to him for translation help.

"The dog's name is Rico," Marco said, then turned to the detective. "Commissario, most of the people here are

English speakers. It might be easier for everyone if we could talk in English."

"Not a problem," he said, nodding. "I'm fluent. I'm Commissario Bruno. And you are?"

"I'm Marco Columbo. This is my wife, Rosa. We own the villa and run the cooking school."

"Yes, La Bella Vita," he said, glancing around. "I've heard about this place and have always wanted to see it." He knelt down over Bronwyn's body, checked for a pulse then got to his feet. "Just not under circumstances like this." He reached into his shirt pocket and grabbed his phone. "I need to make a call. But I will need to speak with all of you." He glanced back and forth at Marco and Rosa. "Is there another room we could use? Some other people will be arriving soon, and they will need room to work."

"Let's use the sitting room," Marco said to Rosa.

She nodded and motioned for everyone to follow her.

"I'll join you in a minute," Commissario Bruno said, reaching down to pet the Newfie before making the call.

Josie and Chef Claire sat down on a couch. They glanced around at the look of shock on everyone's face.

"The Newfie could be Captain's twin," Chef Claire said.

100

"He's beautiful," Josie said. "And it makes me miss Captain even more."

"Yeah, the Goldens have had the same effect on me," Chef Claire said, then frowned. "If it wasn't natural causes, who do you think might have killed her?"

"I have no idea," Josie said. "She was totally self-absorbed but seemed harmless. And what's the deal with her blouse being half-undone and all the lipstick?"

"I don't think you're the only one asking that question," Chef Claire said, nodding across the room where Emerson was giving Georgio a hostile glare. "Emerson seems to think she tarted herself up for Georgio."

"Tarted herself up?" Josie said, raising an eyebrow.

"You know what I mean," Chef Claire said. "Ruby-red lipstick. Big pouty lips. Showing a lot of cleavage. The come-hither look on her face."

"Judging by the expression on her face, if she was getting ready to hook up with Georgio, wouldn't that mean he was standing right in front of her when it happened?" Josie said.

"Yeah, it must," Chef Claire said. "But why would Georgio want to kill her? Since the Kingsleys had decided to take a break from each other, wouldn't it open up the possibility she and Georgio could rekindle what they had before?"

"One would think," Josie said. "Unless Georgio wasn't interested in getting back together with her."

"Maybe Emerson came into the dining room while she was putting her lipstick on and confronted her."

"And then she mocked him with that expression?" Josie said, frowning.

"I guess I can make that work," Chef Claire said. "But Bronwyn said it was Emerson's idea to separate. Why would he care?"

"Maybe it wasn't the fact she was going to start seeing other people that drove Emerson crazy. Maybe he just hated the idea Georgio was the first person she was heading for."

"I don't know," Chef Claire said, shaking her head. "But whoever did it had to have been in a rage, right?"

"To kill somebody out in the open with a dozen other people nearby? Yeah. Either rage or uncontrollable insanity. There wasn't any blood. Did you see any wounds or bruises?"

"No, but I didn't take a good look," Chef Claire said. "Did you?"

"No," Josie said, shaking her head. "Weird, huh?"

"Maybe she was poisoned," Chef Claire said.

"If someone had given her poison, there's no way she would have been smiling like that, right?"

"Unless she was given the poison earlier."

Josie stared at Chef Claire then cocked her head.

"You mean, maybe she was poisoned during dinner?"

"I don't know," Chef Claire said. "I'm just spitballing here."

"She died from something she ate tonight?" Josie said. "Now, there's a cheery thought."

"Anything is possible," Chef Claire said, shrugging. "You didn't happen to drop your pasta dough on the floor this afternoon, did you?"

"Funny. Real funny," Josie said, gently punching Chef Claire on the arm. "Feel my forehead."

"What?"

"Do I feel hot?"

"Are you feeling sick?"

"No, but if Bronwyn got poisoned at dinner, I might be in a world of hurt."

"Because you sampled every dish?"

"Yeah," Josie said. "Maybe it's just taking me longer to feel the effect. I've got a pretty good immune system."

"I doubt very much if you've been poisoned, Josie."

"Feel my head."

Chef Claire shook her head but complied. She placed the back of her hand against Josie's forehead.

"What did you feel?" Josie said.

"A vast emptiness."

Chapter 10

Everyone continued to sit quietly until Commissario Bruno returned a few minutes later. He glanced around then selected a spot in front of the fireplace. He removed a notebook from his pocket and leaned against the mantel. Rico, his Newfie, stretched out in front of him and wagged his tail like a metronome as he surveyed the group.

"They'll be here in a few minutes," he said. "I apologize for bringing Rico along. I was heading back from my place on the north end of the lake when I got the call. Rico loves going to the lake." He leaned down to briefly rub the dog's head then grinned. "Don't you?"

Rico thumped his tail and let loose with a soft woof. Commissario Bruno laughed along with Josie and Chef Claire.

"I love this guy," he said.

"This is a dog house. He's more than welcome," Marco said. "Rosa and I have four Golden Retrievers."

"Nice," the detective said, nodding. "Okay, let's get started. I'm Commissario Bruno. For those of you who aren't Italian, commissario is another word for chief inspector or detective. I work out of the Lake Garda district and on call tonight. A lot of people are off because of the holiday." He flourished a pen and glanced around the room. "Who found the body?"

"I did," Rosa said, raising her hand. "I came out of the kitchen and was heading for the veranda to watch the fireworks when I saw her on the dining room floor."

"Okay," he said, jotting down a note. "What time was this?"

"It couldn't have been more than five minutes before Georgio called the police," Rosa said.

"Georgio?" Commissario Bruno said, glancing around again.

"That's me," Georgio said. "We were all outside on the veranda when we heard Rosa scream."

"And you had just finished dinner, right?"

"Yes," Marco said. "Probably about fifteen minutes earlier."

Everyone nodded in agreement and the detective jotted down another note.

"So, we have a window of approximately twenty minutes from the time she was killed until her body was discovered," Commissario Bruno said.

"Killed?" Emerson said.

"I'm sorry," the cop said. "For now, perhaps a better term would be when she died. And you are?"

"I'm Emerson Kingsley," he said, puffing up. "Bronwyn was my wife."

"I'm so sorry for your loss. You must be devastated."

"Of course, I'm devastated. What makes you think she was killed?"

"A woman in the prime of her life dies suddenly on the dining room floor. Let's call it a hunch."

"That's preposterous," Emerson said with a scowl.

"Perhaps," Commissario Bruno said. "What's your explanation?"

"I don't know," Emerson said. "Maybe it was something she ate."

The group murmured and nervously glanced back and forth at each other.

"I'm missing something," Commissario Bruno said. "What is it?"

"We all made a dish tonight," Betty said.

"I see," the detective said. "Cooking school, right?"

"Yes," Marco said. "Each night we sample dishes the students have prepared."

"Did you serve anything exotic tonight?" Commissario Bruno said, scribbling down another note. "You know, any ingredients tricky to prepare that might cause severe food poisoning?"

"Exotic?" Marco said, then shook his head. "No. Today was pasta day. And we also had salad and a chicken dish."

"And you all ate tonight?" the detective said, scanning everyone's expression. He received nods and shrugs from the group. "Is anyone having any digestive issues? Any unexplained pain or fever?"

This time, everyone shook their head.

"You think she might have been poisoned?" Rosa said.

"The thought did cross my mind," Commissario Bruno said. "Maybe you have a really bad student in the class. Did any of the dishes taste...*off?*"

"No," Marco said. "Actually, they were all quite good."

"Were all the dishes prepared the same way?"

108

"Pretty much," Marco said. "But the students did make their own pasta and sauce."

"I see. No one is feeling any sort of discomfort?" Commissario Bruno said, surveying the group again. Receiving no response, he shifted gears. "Did your wife have any sort of health problems, Mr. Kingsley?"

"None," Emerson said, shaking his head. "Bronwyn took great care of herself."

"Had she been under a lot of stress?" the inspector said, continuing to gently probe.

"Stress?" Emerson said, frowning. "What the heck did she have to be stressed about?"

"I have no idea," Commissario Bruno said. "That's why I asked."

"Sorry," Emerson said, shaking his head. "No, there was nothing in her life causing any stress."

Georgio snorted.

"You got something to say, Georgio?" Emerson said, glaring at him.

"No," Georgio said. "Not a thing, Emerson."

"Spit it out," Emerson said. "You've never been shy about voicing your opinions. Why start now?"

"I merely found your comment about her lack of stress amusing," Georgio said, then took a sip of wine.

"Did you now?" Emerson said. "Then why don't you let the rest of us in on the joke? Since you find my wife's death somehow funny."

"I didn't say that," Georgio snapped, giving Emerson a dark glare. "There's nothing funny about what happened to Bronwyn. What is funny is your cluelessness about what was going on with her. Nothing causing stress in her life? Good one, Emerson."

"Like what?" Emerson said.

"Well, being married to you, for starters," Georgio said.

"Here we go," Josie whispered.

"Shhh," Chef Claire said. "This is about to get good."

"Check out the dog," Josie whispered, nodding in the direction of the Newfie who had his head cocked as he glanced back and forth at Emerson and Georgio.

"He's on the case," Chef Claire said, doing her best not to laugh.

Emerson took a step closer to Georgio and maintained his stare.

"You got something to say about our marriage?"

"I don't think I need to comment," Georgio said. "You can't be clueless."

Emerson flinched before looking at Commissario Bruno.

"Our marriage was fine," Emerson said.

Georgio snorted again.

"Commissario, would you arrest me if I beat the crap out of this guy?" Emerson said, taking another step closer.

"Anything's possible," the detective said. "But let's not try to find out, okay?" He faced Georgio who continued to stare off into the distance as he sipped his wine. "I take it you knew the victim."

"I've known her and Emerson for years," Georgio said. "I do business with Emerson's company from time to time."

"And what do you do?" Commissario Bruno said.

"I'm an inventor."

"Really? That's interesting. What sort of things do you invent?"

"Gadgets, mostly. For around the house," Georgio said. "Occasionally, I do some things with electronics and technology."

"I see," the detective said. "Where were you when you heard Rosa scream?"

"I was outside on the veranda with everyone else," Georgio said.

Commissario Bruno looked around the room and got several confirming nods. Satisfied for the moment, he looked at Josie and Chef Claire.

"Could I have your names please?"

"I'm Josie. This is Chef Claire."

Commissario Bruno jotted their names down then continued.

"Were you also outside when you heard the scream?"

"We all were," Chef Claire said. "Except for Rosa."

He got everyone's name, asked a few follow-up questions, then jotted down a few more notes and shook his head.

"It's most odd," he said, rubbing his eyes as he stifled a yawn. He looked at Emerson who continued his death-stare match with Georgio. "Are you sure your wife didn't have any health issues?"

"If she did, she never shared them with me," Emerson said. "Are you thinking something like a heart attack?"

112

"I don't know what I'm thinking at the moment, sir. Did you see what she ate at dinner?"

"She was sampling lots of different dishes," Betty Smithsonian said, then caught the look the detective was giving her. "I sat across from her at dinner."

"Did you talk to each other during dinner?"

"We did," Betty said, nodding. "Mostly it was just idle chatter. She talked about herself a lot."

"How so?" the detective said.

"She was...how do I say this without sounding mean?"

"I have no idea," Commissario Bruno said. "That's why I asked."

"She was..." Betty said, trailing off again.

"Self-absorbed," Rosa whispered to no one in particular.

"Yes, that's the word," Betty said, staring down at the floor. "I hate to even mention it."

"There's the Canadian coming out," Josie whispered to Chef Claire.

"Yeah, the niceness-gene," Chef Claire said, nodding.

"Bronwyn did spend a lot of time focused on herself," Emerson said. "But that's no reason for anybody to kill her."

"No, it's probably not," Commissario Bruno said. "Did she say anything else?"

"Oh, my," Betty said, shaking her head. "I really don't want to get into this."

"I'm sorry," the detective said. "But it could be important."

Betty nodded then glanced at Emerson before continuing.

"She mentioned her marriage was on the rocks. And she and Emerson had decided to take a break from each other."

"Really?" Georgio said, staring at Betty.

"She told you?" Emerson said, surprised by the news.

"She did."

"I suppose she told the rest of you as well," Emerson said, looking around the room.

"Not me," Georgio said.

"I heard her tell Betty," Lance, the surfer dude, said. "I was sitting nearby."

"I can't believe she told you," Emerson said. "We had only decided to do it right before dinner."

"How did you take the news?" Commissario Bruno said.

"Nice try, Inspector," Emerson said, glaring at the cop. "My wife and I decide to separate, and an hour later I kill her?"

"Infer what you like, sir. I merely asked how you took the news."

"Since the separation was my idea, I was fine with it," Emerson said with a shrug. "And I certainly didn't kill her." He focused on Georgio. "Why don't you ask Lover Boy over there if he had anything to do with it?"

"Stuff a sock in it, Emerson," Georgio said, his voice rising. "Why on earth would I want to hurt Bronwyn? Especially since we were about to…"

"About to do what?" Commissario Bruno said.

"Great question, Inspector," Emerson said, still staring at the inventor. "Finish your thought, Georgio."

Georgio sat quietly for several moments before responding.

"We talked this afternoon about the possibility of trying again," he said, then focused on the detective. "Bronwyn and I used to be in a relationship. In fact, she left me for him."

"I knew it," Emerson said. "You've been trying to get her back for months."

Natalie grunted and emitted what sounded like a low guttural growl.

"Not really," Georgio said, shaking his head. "But it was pretty clear how unhappy she was. This afternoon, she said she was thinking about leaving you and would let me know soon." Then he teared up and began to sob. "But she never got the chance."

Betty reached out and draped an arm around his shoulders to comfort him.

"Leave *me* for *you*?" Emerson said, laughing. "Who's being self-absorbed now?"

"Emerson, please," Rosa said, shaking her head at him. "Not now."

"I'm sorry, Rosa," Emerson said. "But come on, let's get real here. There's no way Bronwyn was going to go back to that philanderer." He nodded in the general direction of Lance. "The surfer dude had a better shot with her than Georgio."

"Please, leave me out of this," Lance said. "I'm sorry for your loss, but it has nothing to do with me."

Commissario Bruno listened closely to the young man's comment, seemed satisfied, then turned to Donato and Maria Peccati, the Italian couple with the catering company. He soon realized they weren't comfortable answering his questions in English, so he switched to Italian. They conversed for a few minutes until the detective smiled and nodded at them. He knelt down to rub the Newfie's head, and a concentrated stare emerged. It lasted until everyone heard a loud knock. The inspector stood and looked at the front door.

"That will be my people," Commissario Bruno said. "I think we're done here for tonight. But I'm sure I'll have more questions after we get an idea of what happened to her. You'll all be here for the rest of the week, correct?"

"Do we have a choice?" Emerson said.

"Uh, no," the detective said. "I'm afraid I'm going to have to insist none of you leave until I give you the go ahead."

"We understand, Commissario," Marco said, following the detective to the door.

"Okay," Josie said, getting to her feet. "I think I'm ready to call it a night. Are you going to bed?"

"I thought I might go say hi to the Goldens," Chef Claire said.

"What a good idea," Josie said, then glanced over at Rosa. "Would it be okay to introduce the Newfie to your dogs?"

"Sure," Rosa said. "In fact, I'll go with you. I could use a little four-legged companionship at the moment."

"Great," Josie said, then knelt down in front of the dog. "What do you say, Rico? You want a snack?"

The dog cocked his head at her but didn't budge.

"Odd," Josie said. "That question works like a charm at home."

"Think it through, Josie," Chef Claire said.

"What?"

"The dog's Italian," Chef Claire said.

"Oh, of course. Duh," she said, then turned to Rosa. "How do you say snack in Italian?"

"Merenda," Rosa said, giving the Newfie a loving stare.

"Thanks," Josie said. "*Merenda*, Rico?"

The dog stood and wagged his tail furiously as he stared at Josie with an expectant look.

"How about that?" Josie said, glancing back and forth at Chef Claire and Rosa. "I'm fluent."

Chapter 11

Josie knocked softly then opened the connecting door and poked her head in. Chef Claire, like Josie, was already in her pajamas.

"Are you ready?" Josie said, waving her phone in the air.

"I am," Chef Claire said. "Come on in."

Josie sat down and placed her phone on the end table separating two large, overstuffed chairs. Chef Claire sat down in the other and Josie made the call and put the phone on speaker.

"I was wondering if you guys were going to call tonight."

"Hey," Josie said.

"Hi, Suzy."

"Hi, guys. How's it going?" Suzy said.

"Well, we've had better nights," Josie said. "How are the dogs?"

"They're great," Suzy said. "At the moment, all five are fighting for space on the bed. Captain is winning."

"Five?" Josie said.

"Queen is here," Suzy said. "My mom decided to stay with me while you guys were away."

"Nice," Chef Claire said. "Tell her we said hi."

"Will do. What happened to ruin your night?"

Josie and Chef Claire looked at each other. Chef Claire motioned for Josie to proceed.

"One of the students at the cooking school died tonight," Josie said.

"Died? I hope it wasn't something she ate because that would be really bad PR for the school."

"We're not sure what happened to her," Josie said. "She collapsed right after dinner."

"Weird. Heart attack?"

"I suppose anything is possible," Josie said. "The cops don't have a clue yet. There were no signs of a struggle, no blood or wounds."

"Probably natural causes, right?" Suzy said. "Was she old?"

"Early-thirties at most and very fit. Bronwyn said she spent a couple of hours a day working out," Josie said. "It seems unlikely it was natural causes."

"Unless she had some sort of health problem nobody knew about," Suzy said.

"Yeah," Josie said. "We were wondering the same thing."

"Food poisoning wouldn't cause her to drop dead like that," Suzy said. "What did you have for dinner?"

"We made pasta today," Josie said. "I did rigatoni with a mushroom ragu. A total knee-buckler."

"Nice," Suzy said. "Did everybody in class make a dish?"

"Yeah," Josie said. "Ten different pastas. It was a ton of food."

"That's all you had?" Suzy said.

"No, Chef Claire, being the teacher's pet, offered to make the salad," Josie said, laughing.

"Shut it," Chef Claire said.

"And Marco and Rosa, they own the villa and run the school, did an amazing chicken dish in a light cream sauce," Josie said.

"Yum," Suzy said.

"It was incredible," Josie said. "They used cognac and mint in the sauce."

"I've tried pairing those two before but never got it right," Suzy said.

"I'll see if I can get the recipe," Josie said.

"Can we please focus here, guys?" Chef Claire said.

"Sorry," Josie said. "So, anyway, that was our night."

"Who else is at the school?" Suzy said.

"Well, there's an Italian couple who run a catering company and some surfer dude out of California," Josie said.

"What the heck is he doing there?"

"According to him, trying to get his parents off his back," Chef Claire said. "Oh, and there's a woman from Ottawa here who's been at C's several times. Do you remember a woman by the name of Betty Smithsonian?"

"Short, attractive blonde somewhere in her forties?" Suzy said.

"That's her," Chef Claire said.

"Yeah, I remember Betty," Suzy said. "She's nice."

"She is," Josie said. "The woman who died was the wife of somebody named Emerson Kingsley. He has some sort of manufacturing company on the west coast."

"Are the cops looking at him for it?" Suzy said.

"I'm not sure they're looking at anybody at the moment," Chef Claire said. "But he did tell her this afternoon he wanted to take a break."

"That's interesting," Suzy said.

Josie and Chef Claire frowned when they heard the familiar crinkle of foil through the phone.

"You're eating bite-sized Snickers, aren't you?" Josie said.

"Maybe."

"Well, since you can't have any booze, I guess chocolate is a good fallback," Chef Claire said. "How are you feeling?"

"Physically, I feel good," Suzy said. "No morning sickness to speak of. And the doctor says everything is fine. Mentally, I'm getting a little stronger every day."

"Just don't overdo it," Josie said.

"Don't worry. My mom is constantly hovering," Suzy said. "Who else is at the school?"

"You'll never guess," Josie said, laughing.

"Give me a hint."

"Vegas. Russia. Vodka," Josie said.

Chef Claire and Josie waiting out a long silence.

"Natalie?" Suzy said.

"Yup," Josie said.

"I can't believe it. What the heck is she doing at cooking school?"

"She's here with Georgio," Chef Claire said.

"Boyfriend?"

"TBD," Chef Claire said. "They're definitely an odd couple."

"Well, we are talking about Natalie," Suzy said. "Judging by the name, I'm gonna guess he's Italian."

"He is," Josie said. "And he's a total womanizer who used to have a thing with the victim. Based on what we heard tonight, it sounds like they were thinking about giving it another shot."

"Did the husband know?" Suzy said over another loud crinkle.

"He definitely had his suspicions," Chef Claire said.

"It sounds like a motive to me," Suzy said.

"Yeah, we thought the same thing," Josie said. "But there was nothing wrong with the body. And she was fine all throughout dinner."

"Definitely strange," Suzy said. "What does this guy Georgio do?"

124

"That's where it gets even more interesting," Chef Claire said. "He's an inventor."

"Really?"

"Yeah, he invented a pasta maker you aren't going to believe," Chef Claire said. "Georgio gave all the students one today. So, we'll have two at the house. It's incredible."

"You and your kitchen gadgets," Suzy said, laughing.

"I'm not joking," Chef Claire said, glancing at Josie. "Am I wrong?"

"No," Josie said. "It's amazing."

"Do you think the inventor might have rigged the victim's machine with some sort of poison?" Suzy said.

Chef Claire and Josie looked at each other before shaking their heads.

"No, I don't think it's possible," Chef Claire said. "The pasta makers were sitting at different workstations, and we weren't assigned spots."

"I agree," Josie said. "It was totally random who got what machine."

"Maybe he wasn't targeting the victim," Suzy said. "Maybe he just wanted to see if whatever it is worked."

Chef Claire and Josie stared at each other again as they processed Suzy's comment.

"Nah," Chef Claire said, shaking her head. "Georgio is one of the investors in the place. And he definitely has a vested interest in its success."

"Yeah, he wouldn't do anything that might create bad publicity," Josie said.

"Okay. Makes sense," Suzy said. "The guy invents kitchen gadgets? I guess there's a ton of ways to make a living, huh?"

"Apparently, kitchen gadgets aren't the only thing he invents," Josie said.

"What else?" Suzy said.

"Rumor has it he's also involved in weapon systems," Josie said.

"And also using technology for, shall we say, less than moral purposes," Chef Claire said.

"Who did you hear this rumor from?" Suzy said.

"Bronwyn. The victim," Josie said.

"And Rosa also mentioned it," Chef Claire said.

"People know this guy is an arms dealer and he's out walking around?"

"Yeah," Josie said. "Our best guess is that he might be working both sides of the street. You know, selling to everybody."

"Including the U.S.?"

"Could be," Chef Claire said.

"Maybe nobody has been able to catch him yet," Suzy said.

"Who knows?" Josie said. "And I doubt if we're going to be able to find out. I certainly don't want to stick my nose into something like that."

"I guess we're different that way," Suzy said, laughing.

"Touché," Josie said, laughing along.

"I do have one idea," Suzy said. "It's a longshot, but it might be worth the effort."

"Why am I getting a bad feeling about this?" Josie said to Chef Claire.

"Yeah, definitely a déjà vu moment," Chef Claire said, shaking her head. "Okay, Snoopmeister, what have you got?"

"It would be nice if you could confirm what this guy is up to," Suzy said.

"I can live without knowing," Josie said.

"No, hang on," Chef Claire said. "Let's hear her out."

"Thank you, Chef Claire," Suzy said. "If this guy is doing what you say he is, he must be on the government's radar."

"Sure," Josie said. "Let's just call the Feds and ask them. I'm sure they'll be happy to confirm it."

"There's no need to get snarky," Suzy said. "And you don't need the whole government. All you need is one person who works in the right place."

"And I suppose you have someone in mind?" Josie said.

"I do," Suzy said. "Do you remember Agent Tompkins?"

"The FBI agent who had the hots for Chef Claire?"

"I remember him," Chef Claire said, beaming. "That was back when we were dealing with the dog smuggling operation. The people involved were stealing technology, right?"

"That's the one," Suzy said. "And he was totally smitten with you. The last I heard he's been promoted. But I think he's still involved with technology-piracy and espionage."

"And you think I should just call him and ask if he knows who Georgio is?" Chef Claire said.

"Why not?" Suzy said. "It's just a phone call. And who knows, maybe he'll ask you out to dinner."

128

"Funny," Chef Claire said, then glanced at Josie. "I guess it couldn't hurt, right?"

"As long as the phone call is as far as it goes," Josie said. "I don't want anything to get in the way of cooking school."

"I think it's too late to start worrying about that," Chef Claire said.

"Yeah," Josie said, nodding. "You might be right."

"You wouldn't happen to have his number, would you?" Chef Claire said.

"I got it right here," Suzy said. "You got something to write with?"

Chef Claire jotted down the number then settled back into her chair.

"How much are you guys missing the dogs?" Suzy said.

"It was terrible the first few days," Josie said. "But we're getting our daily fix now that we're here."

"The owners have a dog?" Suzy said.

"Four Goldens," Chef Claire said.

"Wow. That's great," Suzy said.

"And the detective who was here tonight brought his Newfie with him," Josie said.

129

"He brought his dog to a murder investigation?" Suzy said. "I like this guy already."

"He was on his way home from the lake when he got the call," Josie said. "The dog could be Captain's twin."

"Captain isn't going to like the fact you're two-timing him," Suzy said.

"Yeah, you should probably keep it to yourself," Josie said. "Okay, it's way past our bedtime, and we have class in the morning."

"You're still having class tomorrow?" Suzy said. "After somebody died tonight?"

"Marco and Rosa discussed it with everyone. We decided to have class and see how it goes," Chef Claire said. "Before he left, the detective said it looks like she died of natural causes, so nobody thought it was enough of a reason to cancel."

"And Marco and Rosa didn't seem very happy about the prospect of having to refund everyone's money," Josie said.

"No, they certainly didn't," Chef Claire said with a frown.

"Okay, let me know how your chat with Agent Tompkins goes," Suzy said.

"Will do," Chef Claire said. "We'll give you a call."

"And don't play too hard to get," Suzy said.

"You're really not as funny as you think you are," Chef Claire said.

"I think we both know that's not true," Suzy deadpanned. "Later."

She ended the call, and Josie turned her phone off then arched her back.

"Do you buy the natural causes explanation?" Chef Claire said.

"For now, I think I do," Josie said. "Stuff like that happens."

"Sudden death," Chef Claire said. "Like what happened to Max, right?"

"Yeah," Josie said, tearing up. "But she sounded good."

"She did," Chef Claire said, handing Josie a box of tissues. "She's going to be okay."

"I still can't believe it," Josie said. "Your husband gets run over by a bus on your honeymoon."

"She's going to be fine, Josie," Chef Claire said.

"Yeah, I know. But she's going to be a single mom."

"She is," Chef Claire said, reaching for a tissue. "But she'll never be alone."

"No, she certainly won't."

Chapter 12

Stifling a deep yawn, he reached for his coffee and took a long sip. Reacting to its bitterness, he got up to make a fresh pot. Since he was going to be here for at least a couple more hours, he was going to need all the help he could get. After pulling a twelve by twelve – twelve consecutive days of at least twelve hours each – he was finding it increasingly harder to muster and maintain the level of concentration he needed.

Just as the coffeemaker began gurgling, his phone began playing a familiar song. He smiled and hummed along as he always did when he heard the ringtone; Warren Zevon's *Lawyers, Guns, and Money*. The ringtone, downloaded for a buck, had been a recent gag birthday gift from his staff. The song about a young man on the run and begging his father to send lawyers, guns, and money was a funny, yet stark, reminder of what he did for a living. Either the number of people needing one or all of those three was increasing, or the explosion of technology had brought to the surface how many people were out there trying to create chaos. The answer to how many there were really didn't matter. What did was that there were enough people like him trying to stop them. Somebody had to do it. And he had raised his hand.

He waited for the chorus to finish then answered.

"Agent Tompkins," he said, not even bothering to try hiding his fatigue.

"Hi, Agent Tompkins."

"Who is this?" he said, frowning.

"It's Chef Claire."

"Chef Claire? From Clay Bay?"

"The one and only. Josie's here with me. We have you on speaker."

"Wow," Agent Tompkins said, his mood improving by the second. "It's so good to hear from you."

"Are the bad guys winning?" Chef Claire said, turning coy.

"Are we on or off the record?" he said, playing along.

"Uh, on, I guess."

"Then no comment. What's going on?"

"Suzy gave us your number. I hope you don't mind us calling."

"No, not at all," Agent Tompkins said. "I was sorry to hear about what happened to her husband. How's she holding up?"

"She's doing better," Chef Claire said. "Hey, how did you know?"

"I work for the FBI."

"Why doesn't that make me feel better?" Josie said.

"Relax, Josie," he said, laughing. "I called Chief Abrams a couple of weeks ago and asked him to keep an eye out for a guy we think might be smuggling some bad stuff across the border up there."

"Define bad stuff," Josie said.

"Again, no comment. How can I help you guys?"

"Well, this is probably going to sound a little strange," Chef Claire said. "But we were wondering if you're familiar with a man named Georgio Russo?"

"Georgio Russo?" Agent Tompkins said, stunned by the question.

"I'm going to guess from your reaction you know who he is," Chef Claire said.

"Yes, I'm very familiar with Inspector Psycho."

"I beg your pardon?" Chef Claire said.

135

"It's one of the Bureau's nicknames for Georgio. Inspector Psycho. The Mad Inventor. General Germ. Take your pick."

"So, the rumors about him are true?" Josie said.

"Hang on," Agent Tompkins said, getting up to pour himself a cup of fresh coffee. He sat back down and stifled a yawn. "Let's back up a bit. Why on earth are you asking about Georgio Russo?"

"Well, we're sort of spending the week with him," Chef Claire said.

"You're at La Bella Vita?" Agent Tompkins blurted, then kicked himself under the desk.

He waited out a long silence.

"How the heck did you know where we are?" Chef Claire whispered.

"Forget I said anything," he said.

"Are you following us, Agent Tompkins?" Josie said, her voice rising.

"No, of course not," he said.

"Then how the heck did you know we were here?" Chef Claire said, pressing the point.

"Think it through," he said, shaking his head at his mistake.

He waited out another long silence.

"You're tracking Georgio, aren't you?" Chef Claire said. "That's it, isn't it?"

"Georgio has been on our radar for a long time," he said eventually.

"But if you're following him and know he's here at the villa, it must mean you've got an undercover agent here as well," Chef Claire said.

"I can't comment on that," Agent Tompkins said, realizing just how badly he needed to get some sleep. "And I shouldn't have said anything. That was my mistake."

"What has this guy done?" Josie said.

"He's done a lot of things," Agent Tompkins said. "Unfortunately, nobody has been able to catch him doing them." He shook off his self-anger and forced himself to focus. "Why are you calling asking about Georgio?"

"Somebody died at the villa tonight," Chef Claire said. "And based on some of the things we heard about Georgio, we couldn't help but wonder if he might have somehow been involved."

"Who died?" Agent Tompkins said, now all business. He leaned forward and placed his elbows on his desk as he waited for the response.

"A woman by the name of Bronwyn Kingsley," Josie said.

"Kingsley's wife is dead?" he said, staring down at the phone.

"Oh, you know who they are, too?" Chef Claire said.

"Nothing gets past you."

"Shut it."

"How did she die?" Agent Tompkins said.

"That's the weird part," Chef Claire said. "She dropped dead right after dinner tonight."

"I see," he said. "But no one else was hurt, right?"

"You mean like your undercover agent?" Josie said.

"Let it go, Josie," he snapped.

"No, just Bronwyn," Chef Claire said. "And it looks like the cops are leaning toward natural causes."

"I see," he said. "But I have my doubts."

"What sort of stuff does this guy Georgio do?" Chef Claire said.

"You mean, apart from inventing pasta makers?" he said.

"You know about the pasta maker?" Chef Claire said. "That was fast."

"All it would take is one phone call from his undercover guy," Josie said.

"Yeah, I suppose you're right," Chef Claire said.

"Josie, knock it off," he said. "You're lucky I can't reach through the phone."

"Oh, enhanced interrogation," Josie deadpanned. "I'm so glad you have something to fall back on."

"Stop," Chef Claire said, laughing.

Agent Tompkins took a few seconds to compose himself before continuing.

"Just do me a favor, okay?"

"We'll do our best," Chef Claire said.

"Go to class, take in the scenery, and have a lot of good food and wine," he said. "And that's it. Stay out of whatever situation plays out."

"Are we in any danger?" Chef Claire said.

"You two? No, not if you stay out of the way. You'd be the last people Georgio would want to hurt. Knowing what we know about him, I'm sure the things he'd like to do with you and Josie fall under a different category."

"Got it," Chef Claire said.

"How did the Kingsley woman die?"

"Like I said, nobody knows," Chef Claire said. "There wasn't any blood, no visible wounds, no sign of a struggle. Nothing like that at all."

"Okay," Agent Tompkins said. "Look, if there's nothing else, I need to run."

"Thanks for your help," Chef Claire said. "It was good talking to you."

"This call never happened," he said. "But please promise to stay out of the way if anything else happens, okay?"

"Will do," Chef Claire said.

"And if you ever find yourself in D.C., I'd love to take you to dinner."

"And if you're ever in Clay Bay, I'll be happy to cook for you," Chef Claire said.

"Even better," Agent Tompkins said. "But I'm not sure I can come up with a good reason to justify the trip."

"Maybe the smuggling thing you mentioned will pan out," Josie said.

"You haven't changed a bit have you, Josie?" he said.

"It's a little late for that, Agent Tompkins," she said, laughing.

"Enjoy cooking school," he said. "And please be careful."

"Will do," Chef Claire said. "Good night."

She ended the call. Agent Tompkins allowed himself a few moments to think about how good she sounded, and he wondered if she still looked as good as she had a few years ago. Pushing aside all *what might have been* thoughts, he found the number stored in his phone and made the call.

"I was just about to give you a call," the voice said.

"I hear we had a bit of a problem at the villa tonight," Agent Tompkins said.

"How the heck did you know that?"

"I just got a call from Chef Claire and Josie," he said. "You know who I'm talking about, right?"

"Sure. They're a little hard to miss. Why did they call you?"

"They had some questions about our friend," he said.

"Okay. But how do you know them?"

"I met them a couple of years ago when I was working another case," Agent Tompkins said. "I gave them my card and told them to call me if they ever needed my help."

"They're suspicious about Georgio?"

"I think they're just being nosy," he said. "You won't have any problems with them. We're lucky their other friend isn't there. She's a total snoop. And really good at it."

"Okay."

"But do me a favor," Agent Tompkins said. "Keep an eye on them and out of harm's way."

"I'll do my best."

"She really dropped dead?"

"Yeah. The local cops are leaning toward natural causes. But that's going to change if they decide to do an autopsy."

"What are the odds they won't?"

"I have no idea. It's not like I can insert myself into their investigation."

"No, you can't," Agent Tompkins said. "But this means he might have brought it with him."

"It does. But I have no idea why he decided to kill her. It sounded like they were about to hook up again."

"Any chance Emerson got his hands on it?" he said.

"I seriously doubt it. My gut tells me Emerson is about to be cut out of whatever deal they're working on. And they almost came to blows tonight."

"What about our other friend?"

"Marco?"

"Yeah."

"I'm not positive yet. But I'm pretty sure he's just a dupe who somehow managed to get sucked up in this thing."

"Okay. Well, keep me posted."

"Will do."

"Hey, how's cooking school going?"

"It's really good. Tomorrow we're all helping out preparing the feast."

"Feast?"

"All Saints' Day. It's a national holiday."

"I'm not familiar with it," Agent Tompkins said.

"That's because you haven't stepped inside a church in twenty years."

"I've been busy. What is it?"

"It's the day when all the Catholic saints are celebrated collectively."

"Oh, so it's sort of like Presidents' Day?"

"I doubt if the Vatican would agree with your analogy, but close enough. Good night, Agent Tompkins."

"Yeah, get some sleep."

143

"That's good advice. Maybe you should take it."

Chapter 13

Josie and Chef Claire leaned against one of the kitchen counters sipping cappuccino and working their way through warm muffins the staff had made. Josie swallowed a bite and nodded her appreciation before glancing over at Chef Claire who was holding up her muffin and examining it as if it were some sort of lab specimen.

"Incredible, huh?" Josie said, topping off their coffees.

"Yeah, they're great," Chef Claire said, still inspecting her muffin.

"Are you going to eat it or interrogate it?"

"I'm checking out the color and texture."

"I like the raisins and walnuts," Josie said. "And the pepper is a nice touch. It makes them pop. But I'm getting something else I can't quite put my finger on."

"It's red wine," Chef Claire said, finally sliding the last of the muffin into her mouth. "Marco said it's one of the traditional items he and Rosa serve on All Saints' Day."

"Don't forget to get the recipe," Josie said, reaching for another.

"Already on my list," Chef Claire said, then nodded at the entrance to the kitchen where Georgio was huddled with Marco and engaged in an intense, whispered conversation.

"I'd love to know what they're talking about," Josie said, then glanced around the kitchen where the others were chatting in hushed tones. "In fact, I'd like to know what everybody is talking about."

"They're probably wondering if Marco might cancel class today. Or maybe even the rest of the week."

"The thought crossed my mind as well," Josie said. "But if he had, we probably wouldn't have gotten these muffins. These are amazing. Besides, canceling the rest of the week would mean we'd all be getting refunds."

"I suppose," Chef Claire said, over the top of her cup. "And most people hate giving money back."

"Especially people who might have already spent it?" Josie whispered.

"Great minds think alike," Chef Claire said, nodding as she glanced at the doorway where Georgio and Marco were still whispering to each other. "You think Marco and Rosa might be having financial troubles?"

"I think it's possible," Josie said. "And if this guy Georgio is involved in even half the stuff Agent Tompkins hinted at last night, Marco and Rosa must know about it, right?"

"I'd be surprised if they didn't," Chef Claire said.

"And why would anybody bring a guy like him into their business unless they didn't have any other choice?" Josie said.

"Exactly," Chef Claire said. "Eventually, somebody is going to catch Georgio and put him away for a long time."

"They usually do at some point," Josie said, taking another look around the kitchen.

"And when they do, wouldn't anybody doing business with Georgio be in serious trouble? Or at least find themselves having to answer a whole lot of questions?"

"Another good point," Josie said, then turned to Chef Claire with a big grin. "Well, look at us."

"What?"

"We're turning into quite the pair of amateur sleuths," Josie said, gently punching Chef Claire on the shoulder.

"Hanging around Suzy must be rubbing off."

"Sure, sure," Chef Claire deadpanned.

"Good one," Josie said, raising her cup in salute, then leaned in closer to whisper. "So, who do you think Agent Tompkins' undercover agent is?"

"I don't know," Chef Claire said. "I've been going back and forth on it since the call last night. It's driving me nuts."

"Suzy calls it the itch you can't scratch," Josie said.

"Then I guess we should do the logical thing and ask ourselves the question," Chef Claire said.

"What would Suzy do?" Josie said.

"You're on fire this morning," Chef Claire said, laughing.

"Yeah, and on only four hours of sleep," Josie said. "I think we know what Suzy would do."

"Start asking a bunch of questions and annoying the crap out of everybody?"

"That's the one," Josie said, nodding. "I guess it couldn't hurt to try."

"Who do you want to start with?"

"I think the agent might be the surfer dude," Josie said, nodding in his general direction. "I never bought the *my parents made me do it* argument."

"He does seem a little old to be worrying about what his parents think about his life choices."

"But he is a trust fund guy," Josie said. "When you consider that, it starts to make some sense."

"You're talking yourself out of it already?" Chef Claire said, frowning.

"No, just considering all the options," Josie said, making a face at her. "Who do you think it might be?"

"I thought we might start by eliminating people from the list and see who's left."

"I like it."

"Thank you," Chef Claire said. "Well, for starters, I think we can eliminate the Peccati couple."

"The catering folks?" Josie said, glancing at the couple sitting quietly at the kitchen island waiting for class to start. "Good call. I agree. Who else do you want to take off the list?"

"Emerson," Chef Claire said.

"Where is he?"

"I think he went golfing."

"So much for the mourning period," Josie said, shaking her head.

"Maybe he finds solace in wide fairways and fast greens," Chef Claire said. "I'm not ready to remove him from the list of suspects, but if he's in business with Georgio, I seriously doubt if he's working with the FBI."

"No, hang on," Josie said. "Using someone like Emerson would be the ultimate deep-cover operation, right? You know, get right to the source of the problem."

Chef Claire gave the idea some thought before shaking her head.

"Nah, I don't like it," she said. "Rosa said Emerson and Georgio have been working together for years."

"Maybe Emerson has also gotten himself into serious trouble," Josie said. "And the only way to get out of it is by cooperating with the Feds. Yeah, I think it's possible they might have flipped him."

"Flipped him?" Chef Claire said, glancing over with a grin. "Suzy is definitely rubbing off on you."

"It does kind of roll off the tongue," Josie said. "*Flipped* him."

"I think it's a long shot," Chef Claire said, taking another look around the kitchen. "What do you think about Betty?"

150

"Betty? If she's an FBI agent, she missed her calling," Josie said. "She should be an actress."

"She'd be perfect," Chef Claire said. "Nobody would ever suspect her of being a Fed."

"I can't argue with that," Josie said. "But, no. I don't see it. As much as I don't want to believe it, I keep going back to the most logical person."

"Natalie."

"Yeah," Josie said, glancing at Russian woman who was chatting quietly with Betty. "An ex-spy now working for the Feds. I don't have any problem making that work."

"There's only one problem with that theory," Chef Claire said. "From everything we know about her, Natalie loves working on the dark side. I think she's here for another reason."

"Like getting her hands on whatever Georgio's latest weapon is?"

"Yeah," Chef Claire said. "Given her background, I don't think she'd ever agree to work undercover for the U.S. government."

"Do you think she might have been the one who killed Bronwyn?" Josie whispered.

"I think it's possible. But I sure hope she didn't do it. Natalie's kind of weird, but I like her."

"Yeah, me too," Josie said. "Well, that's all the students." Then she glanced at Chef Claire. "Unless you've been holding out on me."

"Oh, you caught me," Chef Claire said, laughing.

"This stuff is harder than it looks," Josie said. "How does she make it look so easy?"

"Suzy has a gift," Chef Claire said, then frowned. "Maybe we're coming at it the wrong way."

"How so?"

"Maybe the undercover agent isn't one of the students," Chef Claire said. "Maybe it's someone inside."

"Inside the villa?" Josie said, giving it some thought. "That's an interesting idea. Marco or Rosa? Or both of them?"

"I sure hope not," Chef Claire said, setting her empty mug down on the counter. "But they did make the decision to bring Georgio in as an investor. I still can't understand why they would do that."

"I like the financial problems angle," Josie said. "You know, black market money. No need to go to the bank for a loan."

"Maybe," Chef Claire said. "How about the guy who runs the staff? What's his name?"

"Enrico," Josie said. "He is always hanging around."

"That's what you want from your staff," Chef Claire said. "But he would be in a great position to overhear all sorts of things."

"He would," Josie said, conceding the point. "I don't know. I'm stuck."

She stared off deep in thought for several moments until Chef Claire noticed.

"What is it?"

"There is one other possibility about who the undercover agent is," Josie whispered. "Or *was*?"

"Bronwyn?" Chef Claire said. "Wow. I hadn't even considered that. You think the Feds had managed to turn her against her husband and ex-boyfriend?"

"And Emerson and Georgio had figured it out," Josie said. "Maybe the fights she and Emerson were having didn't have anything to do with their marriage. And we did run into Georgio coming out of her room the day we arrived."

"Agent Tompkins had a strong reaction when we told him she was dead," Chef Claire said.

"Yeah. I assumed he knew who she was because she was married to Emerson," Josie said. "Maybe there's more to it."

"She seemed to be a self-absorbed trophy wife. What could she have done to get on the Feds' radar?"

"Maybe something in her past surfaced," Josie said, glancing at the doorway where Georgio and Marco were finishing their conversation. "They both look devastated."

"They do," Chef Claire said. "Okay, let's keep an eye out during class and see if we can pick anything up."

"Got it," Josie said. "But for now, I'm going to *pick up* another of those muffins."

"Grab me one while you're there."

Chapter 14

Marco faced the class, sighed loudly, and rocked back and forth on his heels. He glanced at Rosa who was standing next to him. Then he turned back to the group and addressed the elephant in the room.

"Given the tragic events of last night, I know all of you are still wondering what happened to Bronwyn as well as our plans for the rest of the week. Rosa and I discussed it at length last night, and we have decided to continue the classes. Since it appears Bronwyn died from natural causes, while unfortunate, there is no concern for anyone's safety. And since most of you have traveled far and wide to be here, it didn't seem right to deprive you of the chance to learn."

Marco paused and waited until everyone nodded their understanding.

"This is going to be a difficult day for all of us," Rosa said. "And since it is All Saints' Day, followed by All Souls' Day tomorrow, we're asking everyone to keep

Bronwyn in your thoughts and prayers as we move forward."

Again, the group nodded. Marco and Rosa glanced at each other then she gestured for her husband to continue.

"Our schedule for the next two days will be a bit different so that you can enjoy our traditional events. The staff is handling a lot of the cooking today, but you will be expected to prepare two items. Rosa and I will be splitting you into two groups of four. The first session half of you will learn how to make risotto while the other group will be taught how to make a special treat usually only made at this time of year. Pane dei Morti."

"Pane dei Morti?" Lance, the surfer dude said, struggling with the pronunciation.

"Close enough," Marco said, forcing a smile.

"What it's called in English?" Lance said.

"Bread of the Dead," Marco whispered.

"Seems fitting," Lance said, then flushed when the joke fell flat.

"Lance," Betty said, her voice rising as she glared at the surfer. "That was completely uncalled for."

"Sorry."

156

"They're a delicious cookie made on special occasions," Marco said, glaring at Lance. "After lunch, we'll switch, and you'll be taught how to make the other item. We're preparing an incredible feast made even better by your contributions. Be sure to bring your appetite. After dinner, we'll spend the rest of the evening relaxing and drinking some great wine."

"Not the briar patch," Josie whispered to Chef Claire.

"Yeah, let's hope the cops don't show up today with bad news and ruin it," Chef Claire said.

"I'll be handling the risotto lesson while Rosa will be teaching you the ins and outs of making Pane dei Morti. How about Betty and Lance along with Chef Claire and Josie come with me while the rest of you stay here?"

He glanced around then nodded.

"Okay, let's get started."

Marco and his group headed for the far side of the kitchen where a couple of staff members were putting the finishing touches on Marco's work area. He glanced around, nodded he was satisfied, and the staff departed. He spent several minutes going through the history and the basics of making the rice dish then turned everyone loose to try making a simple risotto.

"Don't worry too much about the flavor at this point," he said, after observing their initial efforts. "Try to focus on getting the consistency correct. You're looking for creamy, but al dente rice. And remember to keep stirring."

He took another look at how everyone was doing then headed for Chef Claire.

"This must be boring for you," he said.

"Not at all," Chef Claire said, stirring her dish. "My risotto needs work."

"I seriously doubt it," he said, laughing. "How are you and Josie holding up?"

"You mean about Bronwyn's death?"

"Yeah, it was quite a shock," he said. "To all of us."

"Actually, Josie and I are pretty used to it."

"What?"

"Long story," Chef Claire said with a shrug. "Do you think she died of natural causes?"

"What choice do I have?" he said, glancing away.

"That's an odd comment to make, Marco," Chef Claire said, still focused on her rice.

"Yes, I suppose it was," he said. "But having a murder occur at the villa is the last thing Rosa and I need at the moment."

158

Chef Claire set her wooden spoon down and lowered the heat of the gas burner. She nodded for Marco to follow her as she walked several feet away. She studied his face closely.

"Marco, I'm going to ask you a question you might not like."

"It won't be the first one I've got since last night. Go ahead."

"Are you and Rosa having financial problems?" Chef Claire said without emotion.

Marco's eyes went wide and he massaged his forehead.

"Is it that obvious?" he whispered eventually.

"Both of you seem to be under enormous stress," she said.

"Well, someone did die in our dining room last night," Marco said with a small shrug.

"No, you've been stressed since we got here," Chef Claire said. "C'mon, Marco. We've known each other too long to play games. I used to babysit your kids."

"Yes, you did," he said, smiling at the memory. "Those were simpler times."

"Are you overextended with the villa and the winery?"

159

"Oh, yeah," Marco whispered. "But it was even worse a few years ago."

"Before you brought Georgio in as an investor, right?"

"Yeah. He was here for cooking school, and one night we got talking after too much wine. I opened up about our money problems."

"How did you and Rosa get into trouble?" Chef Claire said.

"We just tried to grow too fast," Marco said. "We should have waited on the winery, but the offer seemed too good to pass up."

"I get it," she said.

"And when Georgio said he had some money laying around he didn't know what to do with, well, it was…"

"Another offer too good to pass up?"

"Yeah, it was," Marco whispered.

"Did you know about how he makes his money? You know, the more nefarious ways?"

"Where did you hear that?" Marco said, raising an eyebrow.

"Rosa made a comment at dinner. And Bronwyn was pretty open about it," Chef Claire said. "The rumors are true, aren't they?"

"I'm sure a lot of them are."

"A lot of the wrong ones as far as you're concerned, right?" Chef Claire said.

"Undoubtedly," Marco said. "Rosa and I are stuck with him for the foreseeable future. He'd be willing to walk away, but we don't have enough to buy him out. And there's no way we can go to a bank given the questions they'd start asking."

"Questions about how Georgio makes some of his money?" Chef Claire said.

"I'm sure it might come up in the conversation at some point."

"If you don't mind me asking, how much did he invest?"

Marco stared at her then shrugged.

"Around three million."

"Ouch."

"That's the word," Marco said, nodding. "It was the dumbest thing we've ever done."

"So, you and Rosa are riding it out and hoping like hell things don't fall apart before you can come up the money to buy him out?"

"Yeah, it's not much of a plan, but apart from selling the place, it's the only one we've got," he said.

"You do know the three million will be the least of your problems if you get caught up in whatever happens to Georgio, right?"

"I do," he said, doing his best not to tear up.

"I'm so sorry, Marco," Chef Claire said, pulling him in close for a long hug.

"Thanks," he said, exhaling loudly. "You don't happen to know anybody with three million laying around, do you?"

"As a matter of fact, I do."

"Really?"

"But there's no way I'm going to suggest it to any of my friends while all this crap is going on," Chef Claire said firmly, maintaining solid eye contact to reinforce her point.

"No, of course not," he said, his hopes dashed. "You don't have any other suggestions for us, do you?"

"Only that you might want to be careful the next few days," she said.

"About what I say?"

"Yes. And who you say it to."

Chapter 15

Josie started to reach for one of the bowls of risotto then changed her mind and pulled her hand back. She sat back in her chair and wiped her mouth then took a sip of wine. Out of the corner of her eye, she caught the look Chef Claire was giving her.

"What?"

"Stop the presses," Chef Claire said, laughing.

"I'm just taking your advice not to fill up on risotto."

"Good call," Chef Claire said, nodding at the platters the staff had placed on the table. "Look at that."

"What kind of fish is it?"

"I'm gonna guess lake trout," Chef Claire said, holding the platter out to Betty who was sitting next to her.

"From Lake Garda?" Josie said.

"I'm sure it is," Chef Claire said, offering the platter to Josie. "It doesn't get any fresher than this."

"It looks delicious," Betty said, then slid a piece into her mouth and savored it. "Oh, my."

"Wow," Josie said, now completely focused on her plate.

"I might need to steal this one for the restaurant," Chef Claire said, shaking her head as she glanced down the table. "You made this dish, didn't you, Marco?"

"I did," he said with a big smile. "I'm glad you like it."

"Garlic butter sauce," Josie said, glancing up briefly. "What's not to like?"

"Have you heard back from the police yet?" Lance said, toying with his food.

"Oh, let's not do this," Emerson said. "We're trying to enjoy dinner."

"I'm sorry," Lance said, stabbing a piece of trout. "It's just so weird."

"People die all the time," Natalie said.

Georgio thought about her comment for a moment then shrugged and resumed his conversation with Emerson.

"Last night they almost came to blows," Josie whispered to Chef Claire. "Tonight, it's like they're best buddies."

"Yeah," Chef Claire said. "They've been whispering since they sat down."

"Maybe they have bigger issues to deal with than worrying about Bronwyn," Josie said.

"Harsh. But I was thinking the same thing," Chef Claire said. "But what the heck is it? It's driving me nuts."

"What's that, Chef Claire?" Betty said, glancing over.

"Oh. There's something in the sauce I can't quite put my finger on," Chef Claire said. "It's driving me nuts."

"Smooth," Josie whispered.

"Shut it."

"I must say I'm a little surprised by those two," Betty said, nodding at Emerson and Georgio who were again huddled in whispered conversation. "Especially the husband. Where's his grief?"

"Good question," Lance said, obviously eavesdropping. He flashed a crocodile smile at her then focused on Emerson. "So, what did you shoot today?"

"What's that?" Emerson said, glancing up. "Oh, seventy-five. I three-putted the last hole from ten feet. I couldn't believe it."

He went back to his conversation with Georgio. Lance shook his head before continuing.

"It's really none of my business, Emerson, but isn't it a bit strange for you to play golf the day after your wife died? And does it really matter if you three-putted?"

"Bronwyn would still be dead if I had made a forty-footer," Emerson said with a shrug.

"Wow," Josie said, staring down at her plate. "Whatever ends up happening here, I sure hope he goes to jail for a long time."

"You got that right," Chef Claire said.

"Aren't we going to talk about what happened last night?" Lance said, addressing the group.

Marco and Rosa both paused from eating and wiped their mouths in tandem.

"What would you like to talk about, Lance?" Marco said without emotion.

"I don't know," Lance said. "But all day everyone has been acting like nothing happened. Like it was all a bad dream."

"We're just trying to put it behind us," Rosa said. "She's in God's hands now."

"How very Catholic of you," Lance said, reaching for his wine glass.

166

"Hey," Marco said, glaring down the table. "Don't even go there, young man."

"Easy, Lance," Betty said. "People grieve in different ways."

"Yeah, and some people don't seem to grieve at all," Lance said, nodding at Emerson and Georgio. "Like those two. Just another day, huh, guys?"

"You have no idea what I'm dealing with or how I'm feeling," Emerson snapped. "And I suggest you keep whatever ill-informed opinions you have to yourself."

"Your behavior is despicable," Lance said, then went back to his dinner.

A long, painful silence filled the dining room and lingered. Josie eventually leaned close to Chef Claire.

"Pass the fish, please," she said, then lowered her voice to a whisper. "What do you think?"

"About Lance being the undercover agent?" Chef Claire said, holding out the platter.

"Yeah."

"If he is, why would he feel the need to push the issue so hard?"

"Maybe Agent Tompkins told him to," Josie said. "Maybe things are at a tipping point."

167

"He certainly tried to get a rise out of Emerson," Chef Claire said, setting the platter down on the table.

"Yeah. And mission accomplished. But Georgio didn't bat an eyelash."

"No, he didn't," Chef Claire said, sneaking a quick glance down the table. "What the heck?"

"What?" Josie said, following her eyes.

"They're shaking hands," Chef Claire said.

"At the dinner table? That's odd."

"That's what I thought," Chef Claire said, reaching for her wine glass. "And as strange as it sounds, it looks like the handshake of two guys who just closed a business deal."

A loud knock on the front door soon followed. One of the servers left the room to answer it. Moments later, he returned followed by Commissario Bruno.

"Good evening," he said, eyeing the various plates on the table. "I've come at a bad time. I'm so sorry to interrupt your dinner."

"It's quite all right, Commissario," Marco said, getting up to shake his hand. "Have you eaten? There's plenty of food."

"Actually, I haven't," the inspector said. "Thanks. But I'll pass for now. Maybe I'll have a little something after we talk."

"Where's your Newfie?" Josie said.

"He's at the house, and I'm sure anxiously waiting for me to get home," Commissario Bruno said. Then he focused on Marco. "I'm afraid I have some bad news."

"Okay," Marco said, sitting down and reaching out to hold Rosa's hand. "What is it?"

"Mrs. Kingsley didn't die of natural causes," the cop said softly.

"I knew it," Lance said to the table.

"Can I ask how you knew that?" Commissario Bruno said.

Lance's face flushed red with embarrassment, and he did his best to stifle a nervous cough.

"It's just a general observation," he managed eventually. "A woman in her prime and in such good shape...well, it seems odd she would have died of natural causes."

"I see," Commissario Bruno said, maintaining a long stare with the surfer before breaking eye contact. "But you're right. It seemed strange to us as well."

169

"Bronwyn was murdered?" Emerson said.

"I'm afraid so, Mr. Kingsley," Commissario Bruno said.

"How?"

"We believe she was poisoned."

Everyone around the table glanced at each other, and soft murmurs filled the room as the news sunk in.

"You believe?" Emerson said, raising an eyebrow.

"Perhaps believe isn't exactly accurate," the detective said. "Let's say we're almost positive."

"Excuse me if it sounds like I'm somehow questioning your ability as a cop, but how can you not be sure?" Emerson said, tossing out the question that sounded a lot like a challenge. He sat back in his chair and folded his arms across his chest.

"Fair question, Mr. Kingsley," Commissario Bruno said, nodding. "I'm not sure I like your tone, but we'll let it go for the moment. The reason we're not positive your wife was poisoned is because we've never seen anything like this before."

"It must have been something in the food," Lance said, just loud enough for everyone else to hear.

"That was our original assumption as well," Commissario Bruno said.

"But not now?" Marco said, still holding Rosa's hand.

"No, it's not," the detective said. "As soon as one of our technicians discovered what we think was the entry point of the poison, we ruled out the food."

"Entry point?" Marco said, frowning. "Where was it?"

"Her eyes," Commissario Bruno said. "There were also trace amounts on her forehead and cheeks, but it's clear that whatever substance killed her entered primarily through her eyes."

"That sounds nuts," Lance said, shaking his head. "But I suppose if you put the stuff on a towel or maybe a handkerchief and snuck up behind her…" He looked around the table when he saw the stares he was getting. "Don't look at me like that. I'm just spitballing here." He focused on the detective. "That sounds logical, doesn't it?"

"It does," Commissario Bruno said, then turned to Marco. "I need to talk with everyone again. Including all the staff who were working last night. I'm sorry to ruin your evening, but it can't be helped."

"I understand," Marco said, glancing at his wife. "Rosa, would you mind telling the folks in the kitchen not to leave until Commissario Bruno gives them the okay?"

She nodded then headed for the kitchen.

"There's only three staff," Marco said to the detective. "And they were all here last night."

"Thank you," Commissario Bruno said, then focused on the group. "I'll be speaking with each of you individually. And I must emphasize again, especially now that the circumstances have changed, none of you can leave the area until I give you the go ahead."

Everyone nodded and the detective looked around again before his eyes settled on Lance.

"I think I'll start with you," Commissario Bruno said to the surfer.

"Why me?"

"Why not?"

Lance gave it some thought then nodded and got to his feet.

"Can I use the sitting room again?" Commissario Bruno said to Marco.

"Of course," Marco said, also standing. "Just let us know when you need the rest of us."

172

"Why don't we wait on the veranda?" Josie said to Chef Claire.

"Good idea."

They headed outside and sat down, staring out at the night sky and distant lights of the town.

"What do you think?" Josie said.

"It has to be Georgio, right?" Chef Claire said, glancing around to make sure they were alone.

"He invented some high-tech poison and decided to try it out on Bronwyn?" Josie said. "A woman he was hoping to get back together with?"

"I know it sounds strange," Chef Claire said. "But the cop said they'd never seen anything like it before. It has to mean it was something Georgio created."

"Yeah," Josie said. "But it doesn't mean he killed her with it."

"Emerson?" Chef Claire whispered.

"Well, he certainly isn't very broken up about her death. And you saw him with Georgio at dinner. It sure looked like they were having a *business* discussion. Maybe Emerson was the one who wanted to try it out before deciding to partner on a deal."

"And if he put the poison on some sort of rag all he needed to do was walk up behind her and hold it to her face," Chef Claire said.

"There's just one problem with that theory," Josie said.

"What's that?"

"If this poison is as powerful as it sounds, wouldn't Emerson, or whoever it was, be worried about getting it on his hands?"

"Good question," Chef Claire said. "I know I'd be worried about it."

"Maybe it was eye drops," Josie said. "She'd been crying after her fight with Emerson. The last thing she would have wanted was to be walking around with red eyes."

"Or perhaps he was wearing something on his hands," Josie said. "There are boxes of rubber gloves in the kitchen. And tons of oven mitts all over the place."

"Interesting theory," Chef Claire said.

"What is?"

Josie and Chef Claire jumped in their chairs, startled.

"Geez, Natalie," Josie said, glaring at her. "How many times have I asked you not to sneak up like that?"

"I really haven't been counting," Natalie said, sliding into a chair and lighting a cigarette.

"How long have you been standing there?" Josie said.

"Long enough," she said with a shrug. "But I share your confusion. It's most perplexing."

"Can I ask you a question?" Josie said.

"You sound like your friend Suzy," Natalie said, blowing a cloud of smoke skyward.

"She does rub off on you," Josie said, nodding before giving her a hard stare. "What are you doing here, Natalie?"

"Learning to cook Italian food," she said. "The same as you."

"C'mon, Natalie," Josie said. "Fess up."

Natalie took another drag and exhaled. She glanced back and forth at both women then shrugged.

"Sometimes, things are exactly the way they look."

"Yeah," Josie said. "But this isn't one of them."

"Perhaps," Natalie said, tapping ash off her cigarette.

"Those things will kill you," Chef Claire said, nodding at the pack.

"In my line of work, cigarettes are way down the list of things that might kill me."

175

"Let's talk about your line of work," Josie said, glancing around to make sure they were still alone.

"There's really not much to talk about," Natalie said. "I used to be a Russian spy. Then I retired and now live in Vegas. But you already know that."

"Doing work for Hedaya," Chef Claire said.

"There's an interesting thought," Josie said. "But why would the owner of a casino send you here?"

"The reason I'm here has nothing to do with Hedaya," Natalie said firmly. "As far as Hedaya knows, I'm on vacation in Italy. Which is true."

"On vacation? With Georgio?" Josie said.

"Yes," Natalie said, exhaling smoke. "But it's turning out to be less enjoyable than I had hoped."

Josie glanced at Chef Claire then stared out at the night sky before continuing.

"Why are you here with Georgio?"

"Because he asked me," Natalie said. "And I foolishly hoped we might be able to reconnect."

"Reconnect?" Chef Claire said.

"Yes. A few years ago, we had what could loosely be described as a relationship."

176

"But from what we've heard, he was hoping to reconnect with Bronwyn," Chef Claire said.

"So I learned soon after I arrived at the villa," Natalie said.

"You didn't know she was going to be here?" Josie said.

"I did not," Natalie said, taking another long drag. "Imagine my surprise."

"Why the heck would Georgio do something like that?" Chef Claire said. "It's so stupid. Not to mention cruel."

"That's Georgio," Natalie said. "A brilliant man with one fatal flaw."

"I take it you weren't very happy when you found out she was here," Josie said.

"Would you be?" Natalie said.

"I'd be a long way from happy," Josie said.

"I'd probably use my bat on him," Chef Claire said, then shrugged. "Speaking metaphorically, of course."

"Of course," Natalie said, almost cracking a smile.

"Did you happen to confront Bronwyn about it?" Josie said, tossing the question out.

"You can do better than that, Josie," Natalie said as a small smile finally emerged. "Is that your way of asking me if I killed her?"

"Yeah, probably not my best work," Josie said. "Actually, I was referring to whether or not the two of you had talked about your common problem."

"The problem of why it's impossible for Georgio, to put it in dog parlance, to stay on the porch?" Natalie said.

"Yeah," Josie said. "That's the one."

"No, we did not. In fact, we did our best to avoid each other as much as possible."

"Who do you think killed her?" Josie said.

"I really don't have a clue," Natalie said. "The whole situation is quite bizarre. But to answer the question I know you're dying to ask, no, it wasn't me. If I was going to kill anybody this week, it would be Georgio, not her."

"Fair point," Josie said, nodding.

"Sure, I get that," Chef Claire said.

"This is probably going to cross the line," Josie said. "But I'm going to ask."

"I'd be disappointed if you didn't," Natalie said.

"I seriously doubt that," Josie said, laughing. "But here goes. Do you know what Georgio does? You know, some of the less-than-legal things he gets involved with?"

"Of course," she said with a shrug. "How do you think we met?"

"Well, I doubt you met on a dating site," Chef Claire said.

"Nefarious-singles dot com?" Josie deadpanned.

All three women laughed. Then they noticed Lance approaching. He came to a stop in front of them.

"Commissario Bruno would like to speak with you next," he said to Natalie.

She got to her feet and slid her pack of cigarettes into her pocket.

"This should be fun," she said.

"Hey, Natalie," Chef Claire said.

"Yes?"

"Since we have the afternoon off tomorrow, we thought we'd go for a drive around the lake. You want to join us?"

"That sounds like fun," Natalie said. "Thank you." Then she looked at Lance. "How was your conversation with the detective?"

"It was about what you'd expect from a cop," Lance said, sitting down in the chair Natalie had vacated.

"Yes," Natalie said. "They all do seem to speak the same language, don't they?"

Chapter 16

Josie sat quietly waiting for the next question. She checked her watch, realized it was almost eleven and draped a leg over her knee in the hope it would keep her from nodding off. Probably not a good idea to fall asleep during questioning. She pulled a chocolate bar from her pocket and held it out to Commissario Bruno who was sitting across from her reviewing his notes.

"Oh, no, thank you," he said, waving off her offer.

"It's good," Josie said, taking a bite. "It's Italian."

"Now, there's a surprise."

"Everybody's a comedian."

"Sorry. I couldn't resist," he said, sitting back in his chair and studying her closely. "I must say, Ms. Court, you're remarkably calm. Most people show all kinds of stress and nervousness when they're being interviewed by the police. But I haven't picked up a trace from you. Your friend, Chef Claire, reacted exactly the same way. It seems odd."

"How so?" Josie said, taking another bite of chocolate.

"You being so calm when I'm asking questions about a murder."

"Well, it's sort of old hat to us by now," Josie said with a shrug.

"I beg your pardon?" Commissario Bruno said, immediately on point.

"Let's just say we've been around our share of murders," Josie said, polishing off the last of the candy bar and stuffing the wrapper into her pocket.

"Really? Do tell."

"How long have you got?"

Commissario Bruno stared at her then set his pen and pad down on the coffee table in front of him.

"How long do you need?"

"Geez, I don't know," Josie said. "A couple of hours at least. But I don't think any of it is relevant, Commissario."

"Why don't you let me be the judge of that?"

Josie gave it some thought then nodded and launched into several of what she considered the more colorful examples of her exploits. The detective's eyes widened as she continued. Eventually, he held up a hand to stop her.

"Hang on," he said, frowning. "You kidnapped a bunch of roosters?"

"Yes. From an illegal cockfight," Josie said. "At first, it looked like we might get deported, but it ended up all right in the end."

"Good for the roosters," Commissario Bruno. "How many times has something like this happened?"

"Are you talking about the number of people who have died while we were around?"

"I am," he said, still frowning.

"Well, let's see," she said, staring off for a moment. "It has to be coming up on a couple dozen."

"Two dozen?"

"Give or take," Josie said. "Now you see why I'm not nervous talking with you."

"And you solved all of the murders?" he said, baffled.

"Actually, Suzy does most of the work," Josie said. "She has a gift for this sort of stuff."

"Suzy?"

"She's our best friend and business partner. Normally, she'd be here with us, but she's pregnant and still recovering from her husband's death."

"Was he one of the two dozen?"

"No," Josie whispered as she blinked back tears. "He got hit by a bus. On their honeymoon."

"I'm so sorry to hear that," Commissario Bruno said, then fell silent. Eventually, he picked up his pen and pad. "Why don't we get back to the situation here?"

"Sure. It's your interview."

"I'm beginning to have my doubts," he said, shaking his head. "Had you ever met the victim before you arrived at the villa?"

"No."

"What was your impression of her?"

"Whatever impression I did have was superficial," Josie said. "We only talked a few times."

"Humor me," Commissario Bruno said.

"Well, she seemed very self-absorbed," Josie said.

"How so?"

"You saw her. She obviously spent a ton of time working on her appearance. But that, by itself, didn't make her self-absorbed."

"No, it doesn't," he said.

"But she was constantly taking selfies," Josie said. "It seemed like every time she did anything, she had to capture the moment. It didn't take long for it to get very annoying."

"So, her habit of taking pictures of herself annoyed you?"

184

"Nice try, Commissario," Josie said, laughing. "I said I got annoyed, not slipped into a murderous rage."

"Fair enough," he said, grinning at her. "Is there anything else about her you remember?"

"She seemed...*unsettled*."

"How so?"

"It was like she was questioning some of the choices she had made," Josie said.

"Like her choice of husband?" he said, reaching for the notepad.

"How could she not question that one? The guy's a total jerk."

"No comment."

"You don't need to comment, Commissario," Josie said. "I'm sure you had him pegged as a jerk as soon as he opened his mouth."

"Again, I'll refrain from comment," he said. "Do you have any idea who might have wanted to kill Mrs. Kingsley?"

"With all due respect, I think I'll keep whatever thoughts I have about what is going on around here to myself, Commissario."

"What makes you think there's something going on?"

"You mean, apart from the dead woman who was found poisoned in the dining room?"

"Fair point," he said, nodding. "So, you do have some ideas?"

"I have mostly questions and vague notions at this point."

"I sense hesitancy on your part to get involved," he said, tapping the notepad with his pen.

"Commissario, I'm here to learn how to be a better cook," Josie said. "And a woman was just murdered. You said yourself you don't have any idea what kind of poison it was. The last thing I want is to start sticking my nose where it doesn't belong and end up being the next person getting a dose of perfumed poison."

"Perfumed?"

"It's a figure of speech, Commissario," Josie said. "Try not to read too much into it."

"Are you sure you wouldn't like to tell me more about your theories?"

"Sorry, Commissario," Josie said, shaking her head. "Figuring out who killed Bronwyn is your job."

"I see," he said, sliding his notepad into his shirt pocket. "Can I ask you a question?"

"You suddenly need permission?"

"This question isn't about the murder," he said.

"Okay. Sure, go ahead," Josie said.

"Are you currently involved with anyone?" Commissario Bruno said, gently tossing the question out.

"Are you flirting with me, Commissario?" Josie said, grinning at him.

The detective flushed red with embarrassment then coughed nervously.

"I guess what they say about American women is true," he said eventually.

"What's that?" Josie said.

"That you don't pull any punches," he said.

"There didn't seem to be any need, Commissario," Josie said, laughing. "You were about as subtle as a truck."

"I apologize," he said. "I shouldn't have brought it up."

"It's okay," Josie said. "And to answer you, no, I'm not involved with anyone at the moment."

"Perhaps we could have dinner sometime?" he said. "There are some wonderful restaurants in the area."

"I'm leaving in a few days, Commissario," Josie said. "And even if we did end up getting along, I don't do long distance. It's too hard."

"Then we can just keep things casual, right?" he said.

"I don't do casual, Commissario," Josie said. "But thanks for the offer. You're a very nice man."

"Thank you," he said, deflated. "Well, I think we're about done here."

"Okay," Josie said, getting to her feet and extending her hand. "Nice talking with you."

"I hope to see you again. Under more pleasant circumstances," he said, returning the handshake.

"You never know," she said. "Oh, by the way, we're going for a drive tomorrow afternoon. That's okay, isn't it?"

"It's fine," he said. "As long as you don't leave the area until we give you the go ahead."

"Got it," Josie said.

"And if you change your mind, be sure and let me know," Commissario Bruno said.

"Change my mind?" she said. "About going out with you or talking about who might have killed Bronwyn?"

"Why both, of course," he said, beaming at her.

"You'll be the first to know, Commissario," she said, giving him an over the shoulder finger wave on her way out of the room.

Musings While I Wander

Italy in October – 3

My original plan was to write this post yesterday, but I got a bit distracted. I won't bore you with the details. Today, I'm going to share a couple of basic recipes I think should be part of everyone's Italian repertoire. Both polenta and risotto are regional staples. Risotto, in particular, holds a high place in Northern Italy cuisine and there's an endless list of variations and ingredients that can be added. The same goes for polenta, a dish similar to grits in the manner it's prepared. But the main ingredient is different. Polenta is made from ground yellow corn while grits are made from ground white corn, also known as hominy.

They are often featured as main courses here in Italy but are frequently used as side dishes in other places, especially in the States. As such, I thought I'd share a few basic recipes to get you started. Give them both a try if you haven't already done so. I think they'll add some delicious variety to your cooking. I suggest you make them pretty much as outlined below the first few times, and after you've mastered the basics, feel free to experiment to your heart's content.

Polenta

Ingredients

- 4 cups water
- 1 teaspoon fine salt
- 1 cup polenta
- 3 tablespoons butter
- divided1/2 cup freshly grated Parmigiano-Reggiano cheese, plus more for garnish

Instructions

- Bring water and salt to a boil in a large saucepan. Pour polenta slowly into boiling water, constantly whisking until all polenta is stirred in. You're looking for a consistency with no lumps.

- Reduce heat to low and simmer, whisk often until the polenta starts to thicken, about 5 minutes. Polenta mixture should still be slightly loose.
- Cover and cook for 30 minutes, whisking every 5 to 6 minutes. If polenta is too thick to whisk, stir with a wooden spoon. Polenta is done when the texture is creamy, and the individual grains are tender.
- Turn off heat and add 2 tablespoons butter into polenta until butter partially melts.
- Add ½ cup of Parmigiano-Reggiano cheese into polenta until cheese has melted.
- Cover and let stand 5 minutes to thicken then stir and taste for salt before transferring to a serving bowl.
- Top polenta with remaining butter and sprinkle grated Parmigiano-Reggiano cheese for garnish.

Risotto Parmigiano

Ingredients

- 1 ½ cups arborio rice
- 5 cups chicken stock

- ½ cup dry white wine
- 1 medium shallot or 1/2 small onion, chopped
- 3 tablespoons whole butter
- 1 tablespoon vegetable oil
- ½ cup Parmesan cheese (grated)
- 1 tablespoon Italian parsley (chopped)
- Salt and pepper to taste

Instructions

- Heat the stock in a medium saucepan, then lower the heat. (But make sure the stock stays hot.)
- In a large, heavy-bottomed saucepan, heat the oil and 1 tablespoon of the butter over medium heat. When the butter has melted, add the chopped shallot or onion. Sauté until slightly translucent. (About 2-3 minutes.)
- Add the rice and stir briskly with a wooden spoon until grains are coated with the oil and melted butter. Sauté for another minute or so, until you pick up a slightly nutty smell.

193

- Add the wine and cook while stirring, until the liquid is fully absorbed.
- Add a ladle of hot chicken stock to the rice and stir until the liquid is fully absorbed. When the rice appears almost dry, add another ladle of stock and repeat the process.
- Keep stirring to prevent scorching, and add the next ladle of stock as soon as the rice is almost dry.
- Continue adding stock, one ladle at a time, for 20 to 30 minutes or until the rice tender but firm to the bite. (If it's crunchy, it's not ready.)
- If you run out of stock before the risotto is done, you can finish the process using hot water, one ladle at a time. Keep stirring.
- Stir in the rest of the butter, the Parmesan, and the parsley, and season to taste with salt and pepper. Or you can sprinkle the parsley and more Parmesan, if desired, as a garnish before serving.

OR!

If you want to eliminate the need to stand over your stove stirring until your arms ache, try this idea. It's certainly not the most traditional method of making risotto, but I won't tell if you won't.

- Saute the onion in butter as outlined above in a large, oven-safe casserole dish with a cover.
- Add the wine and four cups of the chicken stock along with the rice.
- Stir briefly then place the dish into the oven preheated to 350F.
- Bake covered for 45 minutes until the rice is al dente. (most of the liquid should be absorbed by this point.)
- Remove from the oven, then add the Parmesan, butter, salt, pepper, and the remaining cup of chicken stock.
- Stir constantly for 2 to 3 minutes, until the rice is thick and creamy.
- (If you plan on adding additional ingredients such as bacon, sautéed mushrooms, peas, asparagus, whatever, incorporate them into the risotto before stirring.)
- If desired, sprinkle individual servings with more parmesan and garnish with chopped parsley.

Chapter 17

Josie waited until Natalie and Betty got settled then closed the back door and slid into the passenger seat. Chef Claire climbed in behind the wheel and slipped her sunglasses on. She glanced over her shoulder as she started the engine.

"Are we all set?" she said.

"We're good," Betty said, glancing around. She spotted Emerson's yellow Ferrari still sitting in the circular driveway that fronted the villa. "I thought he was going to play golf this afternoon."

"He is," Josie said. "I saw him after class in the dining room eating a sandwich. He said he has a tee time around noon."

"His behavior has been appalling since Bronwyn died," Betty said. "His wife gets killed, and his biggest concern is his golf game."

"Yeah, he's a real saint," Josie said, shaking her head. Then a taxi heading up the access road to the villa got her attention. "Are Marco and Rosa expecting anybody?"

"They've invited some family over," Chef Claire said, watching as the taxi reached the circular drive and came to a skidding stop right behind them. "The taxi's empty. He must be doing a pickup."

"Georgio and Lance are going into town," Natalie said from the backseat. "The surfer has never been here before, and Georgio offered to give him a tour."

"He should stick to surfing," Betty said, laughing. "Did you taste his polenta?"

"I did," Josie said. "It reminded me of the paste we used to use in kindergarten during arts and crafts."

"How do you know what the paste tasted like?" Chef Claire said, glancing over at Josie.

"Long story," Josie said with a shrug.

"Okay," Chef Claire said, laughing. "But you're right, I don't like his chances of becoming a chef."

Georgio and Lance bounded down the front steps and gave them a wave as they climbed into the taxi. The driver put the car in reverse to give himself some room then tore off down the access road.

"Follow that car," Josie deadpanned.

"Not likely," Chef Claire said, slowly accelerating down the access road. "I plan on going home in one piece."

197

She glanced at Betty through the rearview mirror. "You said you've been here before, right?"

"I have," Betty said, leaning forward. "The drive around the lake is beautiful. But I'm not sure we have enough time to make the whole trip today. It's around a hundred miles. We could probably do it in three hours, but that's without stopping."

"I'd like to make some stops," Chef Claire said, making a right onto the main road.

"Me too," Josie said, nodding as she glanced out the window.

"A little sightseeing, maybe do some shopping," Chef Claire said.

"And some eating," Josie said.

"You just had a snack," Chef Claire said, taking a quick glance into the backseat. "How does that sound to you guys?"

"Perfect," Betty said, sitting back in the seat.

"Sounds good," Natalie said.

"What side of the lake should we take, Betty?" Chef Claire said, slowing down as they reached the edge of town.

"Well, the western side is breathtaking, but the road can be tough to drive. You have no idea how winding and narrow it is in parts."

"I could probably ballpark it," Chef Claire said, glancing over at Josie.

"Let it go," Josie said, making a face at her.

"But the drive on the eastern side is also beautiful," Betty said. "Why don't we head north and keep an eye on the time? At some point, we'll just turn around and head back. You probably don't want to be making the drive after dark."

"Good call," Chef Claire said, making a right and heading north.

A few minutes later, they got their first good look at the southern end of the lake that was cobalt blue today. Chef Claire slowed down, and they all looked out over the water and surrounding homes.

"Geez," Josie said, shaking her head. "Everywhere I look is like a postcard."

"You got that right," Chef Claire said.

"It's beautiful," Natalie said, then flinched when a yellow Ferrari screamed past them.

Emerson gave them a quick wave and a tap of the horn as he blew by. The Ferrari soon disappeared from sight.

"What a jerk," Josie said. "I hope he falls in the lake."

"Yes," Betty said. "I understand why Bronwyn was considering another option." Then she caught a glimpse of Natalie's reaction to her comment. "Oh, I'm so sorry, Natalie. That was insensitive on my part."

"Don't worry about it," Natalie said, then stared out at the lake.

"Not that it really matters now, right?" Josie said, glancing into the backseat. "How did your chat with Commissario Bruno go?"

"It was uneventful," Betty said. "But he does seem baffled by the case."

"He is," Natalie said. "But I imagine he'll figure it out soon enough."

"You really think so?" Betty said.

"How hard can it be?" Natalie said, glancing over at her. "It had to be someone staying at the villa. It's a pretty small group."

"Now there's a cheery thought," Josie said. "You really think someone staying at the villa killed her?"

"Of course," Natalie said. "Don't you?"

"Yeah, I do," Josie said, after giving it some thought. "As much as I hate to admit it." She focused on Betty. "Who do you think killed her?"

"Oh, my," Betty said, frowning. "I've been doing everything I can not to think about it."

"C'mon, Betty, fess up," Josie said, laughing. "You're among friends."

"Well, based on everything I've seen on TV and the movies, isn't the spouse always the prime suspect?" Betty said.

"Yes," Josie said. "So, what you're saying is you think Emerson might have done it?"

"No, I'm not saying that at all," Betty said, turning defensive. "I was merely making an observation."

"I like Emerson for it," Chef Claire said.

"Oh, do tell," Natalie said, leaning forward.

"Their marriage was on the rocks, and Bronwyn was already considering the option of getting back together with Georgio..." Chef Claire glanced at Natalie through the rearview mirror. "Sorry, Natalie."

"Forget it," Natalie said. "Continue."

"They live in California, a fifty-fifty state when it comes to divorce, and it's pretty clear Emerson's only concern is himself."

"As was Bronwyn's," Josie said.

"Yeah, definitely two peas in a pod," Chef Claire said. "My best guess is Emerson went ballistic at some point. And since he's like a three-year-old when he doesn't get his way, he lashed out."

"Even though he says the separation was his idea?" Josie said.

"That what he says. It doesn't mean it actually happened that way," Chef Claire said.

"If he couldn't have her, nobody could?" Josie said. "Yeah, I can make the jealousy angle work."

"But why wouldn't he have taken his anger out on Georgio?" Betty said.

"Because he needs Georgio," Chef Claire said. "We watched them at dinner the other night, and it was pretty clear they were discussing a business deal."

"Interesting," Betty said, nodding. "But it's insane. What sort of business deal could be more important than the safety of his wife?"

"I don't know," Chef Claire said, gripping the steering wheel with both hands. "But I'm willing to bet it's a deal with a lot of trailing zeros." Chef Claire paused to glance around at all three of them. "Maybe Emerson isn't quite as well off as he would have us believe."

"Well, look at you," Josie said, laughing. "Our little Sherlock. Suzy would be so proud."

"Shut it."

"It makes sense," Natalie said to no one in particular.

"Do you know what Georgio has been working on lately?" Josie said.

"Apart from the pasta maker?" Natalie said.

"Yeah," Josie said.

"I have no idea," Natalie said. "But I'm sure he's been working on something."

"What are you talking about?" Betty said, frowning.

"Georgio's inventions aren't limited to kitchen gadgets," Josie said.

"And you know this how?" Betty said.

"Bronwyn told us," Chef Claire said.

"Really?" Betty said, surprised. "What sort of things does he invent?"

"Secret things," Natalie said, glancing over.

"Thanks for clearing that up," Betty said.

"Apparently, Georgio *dabbles* in weapon systems and other things despicable people love getting their hands on," Chef Claire said.

"Other things…like an undetectable poison?" Betty whispered.

"Bingo," Natalie said. "Give that woman a cigar."

"Georgio is trying to sell it to Emerson?" Betty said, thoroughly confused. "The very thing that killed his wife?"

"We don't think he's trying to sell it to Emerson," Josie said. "Our best guess is that Georgio wants Emerson to *produce* it."

"I'm not following," Betty said. "Producing it?"

"Yes, in quantity," Chef Claire said. "It sounds like Georgio is basically a lone wolf when it comes to his work. You know, lots of time in the lab coming up with new ideas. And after he has some sort of workable prototype, he needs to partner with people who can make it in quantity."

"And you think Emerson is that person?" Betty said.

"We think he's one of several people Georgio works with," Josie said, then glanced at Natalie. "How are we doing so far?"

"Better than the cops," Natalie said, laughing.

"Did you share your theory with Commissario Bruno?" Betty said.

"Absolutely not," Josie said.

"Why not?"

"Because my plan is also to go home in one piece," Josie said. "If we're right, who knows how this thing might blow up. And while we're very sorry about what happened to Bronwyn, it's still none of our business."

"I see," Betty said. "I suppose that makes sense."

"It makes perfect sense," Natalie said.

"This is probably going to keep me up at night," Betty said. "How should we handle the rest of the week?"

"Stay out of the way," Natalie said. "And wait for the next shoe to drop."

"Geez, not another one," Chef Claire said, staring into the rearview mirror.

"What is it?" Josie said, glancing over her shoulder.

"A bumper rider," Chef Claire said as she slowed down and motioned for the vehicle to pass them.

The vehicle, a black SUV with dark tinted windows, waited for the road to open up a bit then pulled around them.

"It looks like something the cops would drive," Josie said.

"It does," Betty said. "But it doesn't have government plates."

"Maybe it's just someone who values their privacy," Chef Claire said.

"Well, mission accomplished," Josie said. "I couldn't see a thing inside the car."

"They're turning," Chef Claire said, easing her foot off the gas pedal. "Well, how about that? The sign says it's a golf course. Do you think they're meeting Emerson there?"

"Anything's possible," Josie said. "But it's none of our business."

"You're right," Chef Claire said, accelerating past the resort. "What should we do first? Head down to the lake for a look or stop at one of the towns and walk around? Natalie, Betty, what do you think? Hike down to the lake or do some window shopping and maybe grab a snack before heading back to the villa?"

"It's a holiday," Betty said. "Do you think anything will be open?"

"There's only one way to find out," Chef Claire said.

"Don't I get a vote?" Josie said.

"I think we know how you'll vote," Chef Claire said, glancing over.

Chapter 18

They arrived back at the villa just before the sun went down and found Marco and Rosa out on the veranda surrounded by at least two dozen people. The collective conversation was loud and, judging by the number of wine bottles on the table, it appeared they'd been there awhile. Marco spotted them walking up the front steps and waved them over.

"There you are," he said. "Please, join us. Enrico, could you bring some fresh glasses?"

"A glass of wine sounds great," Chef Claire said, giving both Marco and Rosa quick hugs.

"How was your drive?" Marco said, glancing around at all four women.

"It was beautiful," Betty said, sitting down at the table. "The lake is incredible."

"Yes, we love it," Rosa said. "Marco, can you handle the introductions?"

"Of course," he said, tapping his glass to get everyone's attention. "This is Chef Claire, next to her is

208

Josie, Betty, and Natalie. They are all here at the cooking school this week."

He proceeded to quickly work his way around the table introducing everyone. The vast majority of them were family members, primarily cousins, and they smiled and waved then went back to what they'd been doing. The buzz of casual chatter and laughter again soon filled the table.

"We do this every year on All Souls' Day," Marco said. "It's a day for friends and family. Are you hungry?"

"Thanks, but we stopped on our way back and had an early dinner," Chef Claire said.

"There's a ton of food," Rosa said.

"Where's the rest of our group?" Chef Claire said.

"Well, let's see," Marco said. "The Peccatis are spending the night with family about an hour from here. Georgio and Lance got back from town about twenty minutes ago and headed upstairs to shower and change. And Emerson isn't back from the golf course yet."

"We saw him on the road earlier," Chef Claire said. "He was definitely in a hurry."

"He's renting a Ferrari," Marco said, laughing. "You really don't have much choice about being in a hurry when you're driving one of those."

"Fair point," Chef Claire said, glancing up when the server approached carrying four glasses. He poured and passed the glasses around. "Thanks, Enrico." She took a sip and nodded her approval. "This is good."

"It's a Bardolino we produce," Marco said, taking a sip.

"It reminds me of a Valpolicella," Chef Claire said, holding her glass up to the light. "But lighter."

"Very good," Rosa said, beaming at her before glancing at Marco. "She was such a good student. Never missed a thing in class."

"Indeed," Marco said, nodding. "It's the same grape, but because of the soil and climate around here, the Bardolino is lighter and softer than the Valpolicella." He raised his glass in salute to Chef Claire. "And now you're a world-class chef. We're so proud of you."

"Thanks, guys," Chef Claire said, her face flushed red.

"You're such a suck up," Josie deadpanned.

"Shut it."

Everyone glanced at the double doors when Georgio appeared. He took a look around before heading for Marco's end of the table. He gave Natalie a peck on the cheek then sat down in an empty chair between Josie and

Chef Claire. He grinned and gave both of them a quick once-over.

"Good evening, ladies," he said, pouring himself a glass of wine. "How was the drive?"

"Beautiful," Josie said. "How was your day?"

"It was great," Georgio said, nodding. "Lance and I walked the southern end of the lake then had an amazing lunch at a trattoria. We got lucky. There weren't many places open today."

"It was good," Lance said, nodding as he approached the table. He gave the group a wave then sat down next to Betty. "It was a stew with beans and sauerkraut."

"And potatoes and ham," Georgio said, then laughed. "And a whole bunch of garlic."

"Yota," Marco said, glancing at his wife. "They must have gone to Antonio's. Yota is one of their specialties."

"Well, it was fantastic," Georgio said, glancing around. "Emerson's not back from golf yet?"

"No, we haven't seen him," Marco said. "He's probably playing to last light."

"I don't get it," Lance said, shaking his head. "Hitting a little ball then walking after it just so you can hit it again. It's nuts."

"Any crazier than standing on a piece of fiberglass on top of a ten-foot wave?" Georgio said.

"Surfing makes you feel alive," Lance said, shrugging. "Golf is the walk of the dead. My dad plays a lot."

"I've been thinking about taking it up," Marco said. "But it sounds like it takes an awful lot of time. Which I can't spare."

"You got that right," Rosa said, then studied the car making its way up the driveway. "What the heck is he doing back here?"

"Who is it?" Marco said, following her eyes.

"Commissario Bruno," Rosa said, reaching for her wine glass.

"Maybe he has an update," Georgio said.

They watched as he parked his car then hopped out trailed by his Newfie.

"Cool," Josie said. "He brought his dog. Look at him."

"I can't believe how much he looks like Captain," Chef Claire said.

"Yeah, I miss my guy," Josie said, then beamed at the dog who was heading straight for her. "Ciao, Rico." Then she frowned when she noticed the dog was limping. "What's the matter?"

"I think he stepped on something," Commissario Bruno said as he made his way up the steps. "And it's still in there. He won't let me get near it, so I was taking him to the vet."

"But you decided to stop here first?" Josie said with a frown.

"I got a call earlier on my way there," Commissario Bruno said. "And by the time I finished up, the vet was closed."

"He doesn't seem to be in a lot of pain," Josie said, kneeling down in front of the Newfie.

"No, I don't think he is," the detective said, rubbing the dog's head. "But he won't stop chewing and licking his foot. As soon as I finish up here, I'll see if I can find a vet on call for emergencies."

"No need to do that, Commissario," Josie said, getting to her feet. "I have my bag right upstairs."

"You travel with your medical bag?" he said, surprised.

"Always," Josie said. "I'll be right back."

She headed off, and Commissario Bruno watched until she disappeared inside the house. Then he turned to Chef Claire.

"Can I assume she knows what she's doing?" he said, stroking the Newfie's back.

"She's the best," Chef Claire said, then turned to Marco. "Where are your Goldens?"

"They're inside," he said. "But we'll let them out soon."

"Good."

"Would you like something to eat or drink, Commissario?" Rosa said.

"No, I'm good for the moment. Thanks," he said.

"Do you have an update on Bronwyn?" Rosa said.

"No, actually I'm here about a different matter," he said, then stood when he saw Josie return carrying a small black bag. "What do you need me to do?"

"I'll probably need your help holding him still," Josie said, sitting down in front of the dog. "Unless you decide to play nice, Rico."

The dog cocked his head at her and woofed softly.

"Don't give me any sass," she said, laughing as she reached into her bag.

"What the heck is that thing?" Lance said. "Do you moonlight as a coal miner?"

"It's a flashlight," Josie said, all business as she slid the elastic band over her head. "A hands-free flashlight. It's getting dark, and I need to see what I'm doing." She turned the light on and looked at Lance who immediately held his hand up to block the beam. "It's a good one, huh?"

"Yeah, I got it," he said, waving her away.

"Okay," Josie said, glancing around the immediate area. "Let's get him on his side."

"Rico. Stendersi," Commissario Bruno said firmly.

The dog immediately stretched out on the tile.

"Good boy," Josie said. "I assume stendersi is lie down?"

"It is," he said.

"How do you say stay?"

"Restare," the detective said, kneeling down next to the dog.

"Got it," Josie said, reaching into her bag and removing a long pair of tweezers. "Let's do this." She gently grabbed the dog's front left paw, and the Newfie tried to pull it back. She placed a hand on the side of the dog's face and whispered, "Restare, Rico. Restare."

The dog relaxed, and Josie lifted the paw and gently probed. When the dog flinched, she spread the pads apart and focused the light on it.

"Restare," she whispered again. Then she lowered the tweezers and soon removed a long, thin sliver of wood from the paw. She placed the sliver on Commissario Bruno's outstretched palm and tossed the tweezers back into her bag. "Nasty. It was wedged in there pretty deep. How the heck did you manage to do that, Rico?"

"He was chewing on a piece of driftwood he found at the lake. That's probably when he did it."

"Well, he's all better now," Josie said, still examining the paw.

"You're done?" Commissario Bruno said.

"Apart from cleaning it up a bit, yeah," Josie said, reaching into her bag again. She unwrapped a sterile wet-wipe and rubbed it all over the dog's paw. She tossed the used wipe onto the table then turned the light off and placed it back in her bag. The Newfie started licking her hand and she laughed.

"You're very welcome, Rico," she said, getting to her feet. "It doesn't look like it's bleeding, so I'm not going to bandage it. But keep an eye on him. If you notice any

216

blood, or if he keeps limping, let me know and I'll take another look."

"Thank you so much," Commissario Bruno said.

"Happy to do it," she said, sitting back down in her chair.

"What a relief," the detective said. "I hate seeing him in pain."

"I know," Josie said, nodding. "But he's fine. Aren't you, Rico?"

The dog hopped to his feet, his tail wagging furiously. Josie gave him a gentle thump on the side then reached for her wine glass.

"Why are you here, Commissario?" Marco said. "You said you had a different matter to discuss."

"Yes, I do," he said, glancing around the crowded table. "But perhaps we should talk inside."

"Actually, we were just about to eat dessert," Marco said. "And they're all set up in the dining room. We have quite a collection tonight, so we thought we'd make it self-serve."

"Okay," the detective said. "Then why don't you have everyone go inside while we talk out here?"

"Certainly," Marco said, then addressed the group. "If you wouldn't mind, I'd like to ask all of you to head inside to grab some dessert while Commissario Bruno and I talk."

Everyone at the table nodded and got to their feet.

"No, I'd like those of you attending the cooking school to remain," Commissario Bruno said.

"Uh-oh," Josie whispered.

"I don't like the sound of this," Chef Claire said.

"Yeah, I hate missing dessert."

"Funny."

"Enjoy it while you can. It might be the last chance we get to laugh for a while."

Chapter 19

Commissario Bruno poured himself a glass of water and waited until he had everyone's attention.

"There's no easy way to say this, so I'm just going to put it out there. Emerson Kingsley was found dead this afternoon."

He waited out a long round of whispered murmurs, and he looked around the table at the reactions his news provoked.

"What?" Georgio said softly. "How did it happen?"

"His body was discovered on the twelfth green this afternoon," Commissario Bruno said without emotion.

"Heart attack?" Marco said, sounding hopeful.

"Perhaps," the detective said. "But I'm afraid the circumstances look similar to what happened to his wife."

The table fell silent. Marco ran his hands through his hair as he looked at Rosa who sat stunned with her arms folded across her chest.

"There goes dessert," Josie whispered to Chef Claire.

"Yeah, this is bad," Chef Claire said.

"You think he was poisoned?" Georgio said, his voice low and shaky.

"We think it's a distinct possibility," Commissario Bruno said. "And given what happened to Mrs. Kingsley, combined with the fact he was staying here, I need to ask all of you where you were this afternoon."

"We understand, Commissario," Marco said. "Rosa and I have been here all day. We taught class this morning then immediately started preparing tonight's dinner. Family members started showing up around noon, and our staff can confirm we didn't leave the property all day."

"And your staff?" the detective said. "Did any of them leave at any time?"

"No," Marco said. "We were all working in the kitchen. I don't believe anyone left the villa. Did you see anyone leave, Rosa?"

"No," she said, shaking her head.

"How about you?" Commissario Bruno said, glancing at Betty.

"The four of us went for a drive," Betty said, gesturing at the other women. "We headed north on the eastern side of the lake. Actually, Emerson passed us on his way to the golf course."

220

"But you didn't drive to the course, right?" Commissario Bruno said.

"No, we kept going north," Betty said. "We made a couple of stops and did some window shopping. We can give you the names of the stores we went in. I'm sure you can confirm it with the shopkeepers."

"Okay. It should be easy to check," Commissario Bruno said, scribbling in his notepad. He turned to Georgio. "How about you, sir?"

"Lance and I took a taxi into town this afternoon," he said. "We walked around then had lunch at a place called Antonio's."

"Good spot," the detective said, nodding. "I eat there often." He glanced around the table and frowned. "Where's the Italian couple? The ones who run the catering company."

"They're spending All Souls' Day with family down in Verona," Marco said. "They left right after class this morning. They left a contact number if you need it."

"I will," the detective said, jotting down another note. Then he sat down. His Newfie took it as an invitation and plopped his massive head in his lap. Commissario Bruno rubbed the dog's ears as he stared off into the distance. "Strange."

"Who found his body?" Marco said.

"A foursome playing behind him," the detective said. "Given the holiday, the course was pretty much empty today. Mr. Kingsley went out as a single, and he was discovered next to his golf cart."

"Geez," Chef Claire said. "But for someone who loved golf as much as he did, I guess it's not a bad place to go."

"It appears Mr. Kingsley felt the same way," Commissario Bruno said.

"I'm not following," Chef Claire said.

"He died with an enormous smile on his face," the detective said.

"Really?" Georgio said, frowning.

"He was beaming," Commissario Bruno said. "Strangest thing I've ever seen." He exhaled loudly then slapped his thighs and stood. "Okay, I need to handle some paperwork then track down the Peccati couple. If you could give me the number they left, I'll get out of your hair."

"Of course," Marco said, reaching for his phone.

"I need to remind all of you not to leave the area," Commissario Bruno said, glancing around the table.

"I have a flight back to the States on Saturday," Lance said.

"And I fly out on Sunday," Betty said.

"I'll do my best to clear you before the weekend," the detective said. "To clear all of you. I'll be in touch as soon as I know more."

Everyone nodded and he headed down the steps with a wave and the Newfie trailing at his heels. Josie glanced at Chef Claire who was staring down at her glass of wine.

"I think I might head upstairs," Josie said.

"Good idea," Chef Claire said. "Maybe we'll give Suzy a call."

"Great minds think alike," she said, getting to her feet. She looked around the table and forced a smile. "We're going to call it an early night. See you in the morning."

"Good night," Rosa said, giving them a small wave.

They headed inside where the rest of the group were eating dessert and drinking coffee.

"The desserts look amazing," Chef Claire said, coming to a stop next to the table. "What are you going to have?"

"I think I'm going to skip dessert," Josie said.

"What? Are you sick?"

"No," Josie said, giving the table a loving stare.

"What's the matter?"

"I realized something today," Josie said softly.

"Oh, do tell."

"It happened this morning when I was getting dressed."

"I'm gonna need a bit more, Josie."

"I think my days of being able to eat and not worry about gaining weight are over," Josie said with a sad smile.

"It's about time," Chef Claire said, reaching for a cannoli.

"It's tragic."

"Start working out with me," Chef Claire said through a mouthful as she started her climb up the stairs. "It'll be good for you."

"Doubtful," Josie said, following her. She removed her phone from her pocket and made the call. "Hey, it's me. Hang on, I'm going to put you on speaker.

"How's it going?" Suzy said.

"It's been a day," Chef Claire said, opening the door to her room.

They entered and sat down. Josie placed the phone on the end table between their chairs and watched as Chef Claire polished off the last of her cannoli.

"What happened?" Suzy said.

"Somebody else died today," Josie said.

"Really? Who was it?"

"The husband of the woman who was killed the other day," Chef Claire said, folding her legs underneath her.

"Wow," Suzy whispered. "How did it happen?"

"According to the local cop, it looks like he went the same way she did," Chef Claire said.

"He was poisoned?"

"That's what it sounds like," Josie said. "They found his body on the golf course."

"He was poisoned on the golf course?" Suzy said. "Do you know how strange that sounds?"

"It gets stranger," Chef Claire said. "He died with a big smile on his face."

"Maybe he'd just drained a long putt," Suzy said.

"Funny," Josie said. "The cop said he's never seen anything like it. You got any ideas?"

"Well, my first thought is the same person probably killed both of them," Suzy said. "Since they were killed in similar fashion."

"There's just one problem with your theory," Josie said.

"What's that?"

"Everyone's alibi checks out," Josie said. "It doesn't look like anybody staying at the villa could have done it."

"Maybe the person who killed the woman isn't staying there," Suzy said.

"Somebody came to the villa, killed Bronwyn, and slipped out without being seen?" Chef Claire said.

"I suppose it's possible," Josie said, frowning.

"Or one of the alibis is phony," Suzy said.

"They seem pretty airtight," Chef Claire said. "But the cop needs to check out the Peccatis."

"Who are they?" Suzy said.

"The nice Italian couple who run a catering company," Chef Claire said. "But it couldn't be them."

"No, no way," Josie said, shaking her head. "Could it?"

"I seriously doubt it," Chef Claire said.

"What about the inventor?" Suzy said. "You said he was a pretty shady operator."

"Shady operator?" Josie said, laughing. "You've been binging cop shows again, haven't you?"

"Maybe."

"We don't think Georgio killed Bronwyn," Chef Claire said.

"That's right," Suzy said. "You said they were about to rekindle their relationship."

"Yeah, they were," Chef Claire said. "And it looked like Georgio and Emerson were working on some sort of business deal."

"How did your conversation with Agent Tompkins go?" Suzy said.

"It was really strange," Josie said. "As soon as we mentioned we were spending the week with Georgio, he knew exactly where we were. Right down to the name of the villa."

"Really?" Suzy said. "It must mean he has somebody working there from inside."

"That's our take as well," Chef Claire said. "And the Feds definitely want to get something on him they can use."

"It sounds like this guy, Georgio, covers his tracks pretty well," Suzy said. "You got any ideas about who the undercover agent is?"

"We think it has to be the surfer dude. Lance," Josie said. "He spent the day with Georgio."

"Do you feel comfortable asking him?" Suzy said.

"You mean, just go up and ask if he works for the FBI?" Josie said.

"You might want to try something subtler. But that's the general idea."

"I doubt if he'd admit it," Chef Claire said. "But I suppose we could give it a shot."

"Or just let the whole thing go," Suzy said.

"But what if this guy isn't done killing people?" Chef Claire said.

"Now there's a cheery thought," Josie said, shaking her head.

"Just be careful and keep your eyes and ears open," Suzy said. "Have you seen anything suspicious?"

"Not really," Chef Claire said.

"Hang on," Josie said, glancing at Chef Claire. "The black SUV with the tinted windows."

"Of course," Chef Claire said. "I completely forgot."

"What SUV?" Suzy said.

"We went for a drive this afternoon, and this official looking SUV passed us on the road."

"And then it turned into the golf course," Josie said. "Wow. I think we might have found a clue."

"Who was with you in the car?" Suzy said.

"Betty from Ottawa and Natalie," Josie said.

"Well, there goes my theory," Suzy said. "Given her background, Natalie was going to be my choice."

"I don't think she's involved," Josie said.

"Me either," Chef Claire said. "She says she came here to be with Georgio."

"But he was thinking about hooking up with Bronwyn, right?" Suzy said.

"Yeah, he's pretty much been ignoring Natalie the whole week," Josie said. "She's not happy about it, but her anger is focused on him. I could have made the idea she killed Bronwyn work, but she wouldn't have any reason to kill her husband."

"Who would want to kill both of them?" Suzy said. "Since it sounds like they died the same way, it has to be a package deal."

"A package deal?" Chef Claire said. "English, please."

"Somebody needed to take both of them out," Suzy said. "Since they were a couple, killing only one of them wouldn't necessarily fix whatever problem the killer is trying to solve."

"Joint property rights," Josie said, nodding.

229

"Yeah," Suzy said. "Or the business. You said Kingsley had some sort of manufacturing company."

"He did," Josie said, then scowled.

"What?" Chef Claire said.

"What's the matter?" Suzy said.

"Josie's making a face," Chef Claire said. "I'm guessing she has a thought."

"I do. I'm just wondering if it's possible the Feds are trying to pin the murders on Georgio," Josie said.

"Killing two people and then framing him for the murders?" Chef Claire said. "That's despicable."

"It is," Josie said. "But it's clear they want this guy really bad. And since they haven't been able to come up with any evidence, maybe they decided to get nasty."

"Agent Tompkins wouldn't do it," Chef Claire said, shaking her head.

"Even if it ended up saving thousands of lives?" Josie said. "Who knows what sort of crap Georgio is involved with."

"No, he wouldn't do it," Chef Claire said.

"I can make it work," Josie said. "Lance, the FBI surfer dude, goes into town with Georgio, then changes his story at some point. Ends up denying he spent all day with him."

"No," Chef Claire snapped. "If that's the way it ends up playing out, somebody went rogue. Agent Tompkins would never do something like that."

"Okay, okay," Josie said, holding up her hands. "I'll back off."

"Good," Chef Claire said. "New subject, please."

"Ooh, I touched a nerve," Josie said, laughing. "How are the dogs?"

"They're great," Suzy said. "But they miss you."

"The feeling is mutual. How are you feeling?"

"Full at the moment," Suzy said, laughing. "My mom and I just wolfed down a pizza."

"Are you taking your vitamins and getting enough rest?" Chef Claire said.

"Absolutely," Suzy said. "And the staff at the Inn are already babying me."

"Good," Josie said. "Let them."

"Okay, I'll let you guys go," Suzy said. "Be careful."

"Will do," Josie said. "And let us know if you have any brilliant ideas."

"You guys don't need my help," Suzy said. "You can figure it out. Later."

She ended the call and Josie put her phone away.

"Do you think she's right?" Josie said.

"About us being able to figure this out?"

"Yeah."

"I guess there's only one way to find out."

"Or we could just let it go," Josie said.

Chef Claire gave it some thought.

"I suppose we could just play it by ear and see what happens next?"

"Good plan," Josie said, getting to her feet. "Sleep well."

"You too."

"What are we cooking tomorrow?"

"I think it's protein day. Which is good for someone like you who needs to start cutting down on the carbs."

"Funny."

"Yeah, I liked it, too."

Chapter 20

Chef Claire stared out at the view as she sipped her coffee. Josie polished off the last of her breakfast pastry and stretched out on the lounge chair.

"I thought you were cutting back on the carbs," Chef Claire said.

"I am. But it's not like I'm going to go cold turkey. Good morning, Marco."

"Good morning," he said, sitting down across from them. "Did you get some sleep?"

"I did," Chef Claire said, then frowned at him. "Are you okay?"

"Actually," Marco said, running his hands through his hair. "I'm a little rattled."

"I'd be shocked if you weren't," Chef Claire said, setting her cup down. "How's Rosa holding up?"

"Worse than me," he said, exhaling loudly as he stared out at the view. "It's such a beautiful day."

"You sound almost wistful, Marco," Chef Claire said.

"Wistful. I suppose that's close enough," he said, then forced a small laugh. "But I'm sure things will turn around soon. At least, I sure hope they do."

"You're worried about losing the place?" Chef Claire said.

"Only about a dozen times a day."

"I thought you said you were doing a bit better financially," Chef Claire said.

"I lied."

"Why would you do that, Marco?" Chef Claire said.

"Because it's embarrassing," he said, shrugging. "And it's even more embarrassing when I compare how we're doing with your success."

"What on earth are you talking about?" Chef Claire said.

"You know, the student has become the master," Marco said. "But I'm not surprised. You always were special, Chef Claire."

"I'm not so sure about that," Chef Claire said. "How big a hole are you guys in?"

"Oh, it's deep and wide," he said. "And growing."

"Are you sure you can't you go to the banks?" Josie said.

"It's not an option."

"You mentioned investors the other day," Chef Claire said. "Would they be willing to put more money in?"

"We only have the one," Marco said. "And if we were willing to pony up enough equity in the place, he'd probably consider putting in some more. But Rosa's forbidden it."

"Rosa's really worried about where Georgio's money comes from, isn't she?"

"To say the least. She's convinced the authorities are eventually going to catch up with him. And when they do, Rosa says they'll try to recover as much of his money as they can. By whatever means necessary."

"Asset forfeiture," Josie said.

"Exactly," Marco said. "We could easily lose everything."

"And you need three million?" Chef Claire said.

"That's just to buy him out," Marco said. "We also need at least another million for the winery. And I doubt if it's the last infusion of cash it's going to need."

"What's the problem with the winery?" Josie said. "You make excellent wine."

235

"Thanks," Marco said, flashing her a sad smile. "We got into the wine game way too late. In the old days, it seemed like all the good wine came from Italy or France. Then California and Australia started turning out some great stuff. Now, there are hundreds of places producing wine. And a lot of it is excellent."

"Your wine is comparable," Chef Claire said.

"Yes, it is," Marco said. "But we can't make any money on it. There's just too much good local wine in several countries. So, we're stuck."

"How so?" Josie said.

"There's no way we can develop enough market share here, so we're forced to export. Export or die, right? And we can't compete. We either lower the price of our exported wine, or it just sits on the shelf. And when we get the price down to where it does sell, we lose money."

"Can't you just sell the winery and keep the rest of the property?" Chef Claire said.

"It's certainly an option," Marco said. "But it's hard to give up on the dream."

"Better than losing everything," Chef Claire said.

"I'm afraid that's another big problem," Marco said. "The cooking school doesn't generate enough income for us to keep the villa going."

"I was wondering about that," Chef Claire said. "The numbers don't seem to work."

"They don't," Marco said. "The school is a lot of fun, and it's a great marketing tool. At least, we thought it would be. But we don't make a lot on it."

"Geez, Marco," Chef Claire said. "I had no idea you guys were in such a tough spot."

"Yeah, we don't share it with most people," Marco said. "But I would like to speak with you about something."

Marco was about to continue but looked at Josie and paused.

"Should I go?" Josie said, glancing back and forth at them.

"Absolutely not," Chef Claire said. "Whatever you need to talk about, Marco, you can certainly say it in front of Josie."

"Of course," he said, embarrassed. "I'm sorry." He took a few deep breaths and ran his hands through his hair. "Rosa and I have been looking for a way to generate more income at the villa."

"Okay," Chef Claire said.

"And we think the best way to do that is to convert the lower floor of the villa into a restaurant."

Chef Claire thought about the idea then slowly nodded.

"That would work," she said. "You could probably handle a hundred people, maybe more. And easily convert the registration area into a bar."

"We think we can get capacity to one-twenty-five inside," he said. "And we could handle another fifty or so on the veranda. It would be big enough."

"It would," Chef Claire said.

"And we'd like you to join us," Marco said.

"You want me to invest in a restaurant?"

"And be our visiting chef from time to time," he said. "Whatever you can fit into your schedule."

"But primarily you need my money, right?"

"Yes, we do," Marco said softly, then brightened. "But you can see how great it could be."

"I can," Chef Claire said. "It could be very special."

"I'm glad you feel that way," Marco said. "Of course, I don't expect you to answer right away. Take some time to think about it."

"I don't need any time, Marco."

"You don't?"

"No," Chef Claire said. "I'm very flattered, Marco. But the answer is no."

"Just like that?"

"Yeah, just like that," Chef Claire said.

"Can I ask you why?"

"Two reasons, primarily. The first is I'm doing everything I can these days to cut back on work. The second is there's no way I'm getting anywhere near what is happening around here. I'm sorry, Marco. But it's not going to happen."

"Cutting straight to the chase, huh?" Marco said. "You've always been a no-nonsense woman."

"You taught me well, Marco," Chef Claire said softly.

"I'm beginning to think I should have taken more of my own advice."

"I'm sure there are other investors out there," Chef Claire said. "People love owning a piece of a restaurant."

"I thought I had one all lined up," he said, again staring off into the distance.

Josie and Chef Claire looked at each other then they focused on Marco when the penny dropped.

"Emerson?" Chef Claire whispered. "Emerson was going to invest?"

"He was," Marco said, unable to make eye contact.

"Bronwyn mentioned he was thinking about it," Josie said, frowning. "I completely forgot."

"Why would you do that, Marco?" Chef Claire said. "It's obvious he did business with Georgio. Why would his money be any safer to take?"

"He has a corporate structure behind him capable of hiding a lot of things," Marco said.

"Geez, Marco," Chef Claire said, shaking her head. "Rule number one. When you find yourself in a hole, stop digging."

"You sound like Rosa."

"She didn't like it?" Chef Claire said.

"Rosa hated the idea, but we were out of options. Not that it matters now." He got up and forced a smile. "Okay, I need to get ready for class. Thanks for listening, Chef Claire."

"I'm sorry, Marco. If things were different, I might have considered investing. But it's too weird around here right now."

"I understand," he said, then headed inside.

They waited until he disappeared from sight then Chef Claire shrugged at Josie.

"What a mess," Josie said.

"Yeah."

"Was it harder to say no to him than it looked?"

"Not really," Chef Claire said. "I feel bad for them, but there's no way I was going to put myself in the middle of whatever this is. Would you have invested?"

"Not a chance," Josie said, shaking her head. "But I have to say his comment about Rosa has got me thinking."

"Great minds think alike," Chef Claire whispered.

"Do you think it's possible she was the one who killed Emerson?"

"Twenty minutes ago, I would have said there wasn't a chance in hell," Chef Claire said. "But if she thought bringing him in as an investor could be the death knell…people do strange things when they're under enormous pressure."

"And taking both Bronwyn and Emerson out removed the possibility of Marco taking their money," Josie said.

"It did. But I can't wrap my head around the idea of Rosa being capable of murder."

"It's a stretch, but I'm afraid I can make it work," Josie said.

"I can't. Yet," Chef Claire said, then fell silent before finally continuing. "We need more information."

"You want to talk with Commissario Bruno?" Josie said, frowning.

"Absolutely not. It could put us right in the middle of everything. And all we have right now are a bunch of questions and suspicions. We can't prove anything."

"So, what do you want to do?" Josie said.

"I think we should go out for a drink tonight after dinner."

"And?" Josie said, raising an eyebrow.

"And I think we should invite the surfer dude from the FBI to join us," Chef Claire said.

"I like it," Josie said, getting to her feet. "Just try not to make any waves, okay?"

"Really? That's the best you got?"

"It's still early. You know I usually don't hit my stride until around lunch."

Chapter 21

Lance Jones might have been an undercover agent for the FBI, but one thing he definitely wasn't lying about was his love of surfing. Josie had floated a casual question about how he first got started in the sport, and a twenty-minute soliloquy ensued that left both women with blank stares and bobblehead nods. When he finally finished describing the thirty-foot wave he *fell off* on the north shore of Oahu and his subsequent injuries, he tossed back the rest of his wine and got to his feet.

"The next round is on me," he said, heading for the bar.

"That was brutal," Josie said when he was out of earshot.

"You had to ask," Chef Claire said, shaking her head.

"I was simply trying to get the conversation started."

"New topic," Chef Claire said, finishing her wine. "No more surfing talk."

"You're not interested in hearing more about how he was *totally frothing* when he got *slotted* on that thirty-footer?"

"Uh, no."

Lance returned to the table carrying three glasses. He placed them on the table then sat back down and glanced back and forth at them.

"What are we talking about?" he said.

"Uh, cooking," Chef Claire said.

"Oh," he said, obviously disappointed.

"You still want to be a chef?" Josie said.

"I think it's pretty clear by now I have a better chance of becoming a brain surgeon," Lance said, then laughed. "You've tasted my food. It sucks."

"Well...yeah, it kinda does," Josie said with a shrug.

"But you can improve," Chef Claire said. "All it takes is dedication and practice."

"Nah, it's not for me," he said, taking a sip of wine. "Besides, I'm working on something else at the moment."

"Really?" Josie said. "Do tell."

"I can't talk about it," Lance said. "But my folks are gonna love it."

"What do they do?" Chef Claire said.

"They dabble in a lot of things," he said, shrugging. "Cars. Commercial real estate. Investments and portfolio management. Totally boring."

"So, you're bringing them a new deal?"

"Something like that," Lance said.

"How was your day in town?" Josie said.

"It was good," he said, nodding. "Georgio is an interesting guy. Did you know he has over a hundred patents on things he's invented?"

"I did not," Josie said, glancing at Chef Claire.

"I don't know how he does it," he said. "I have a hard enough time coming up with original thoughts much less do anything with them when I do." He glanced at the front door when it opened. "Hey, there's Betty."

He waved and eventually caught her eye. She approached with a big smile.

"Hey, guys," she said. "Mind if I join you?"

"Of course not," Josie said. "Have a seat."

"What would you like to drink?" Lance said, getting to his feet.

"A glass of whatever you guys are drinking would be great. Thanks, Lance," she said, removing her coat and sitting down. "I had to get out of there. Between Marco and Rosa and the staff, the place is like a funeral parlor."

"If people keep dying, it just might become one," Josie said.

"Don't start," Chef Claire said.

"No, think about it," Josie said. "Death is a growth industry. It might be the solution to their problems."

"Problems?" Betty said.

"We shouldn't be talking about it," Chef Claire said.

"Oh, you mean their financial problems," Betty said.

"You know about them?" Chef Claire said.

"Georgio mentioned something about it," Betty said. "It caught me by surprise when he brought it up. He does love to talk."

"But usually only about himself," Josie said.

"Indeed," Betty said. "He seems to be shaken up about what happened to Emerson. Almost more than he was about Bronwyn." Then she frowned. "How did you know about their financial problems?"

Chef Claire glanced at Josie then shrugged and focused on Betty.

"Marco told us," she said. "And he asked me to invest in a new restaurant he and Rosa are thinking about opening."

"I see," Betty said, giving it some thought. "What did you tell him?"

"I told him no."

"Smart woman," Betty said, sitting back in her chair as Lance returned with her drink.

"What did I miss?" he said.

"We were just talking about Marco and Rosa," Betty said.

"They're nice people," he said. "I hope they get their finances sorted out. It would be a pity if they lost the place."

"How the heck do you know?" Chef Claire said, surprised.

"Georgio told me," Lance said, reaching for his glass. "He wouldn't shut up about it."

"What did he say?" Chef Claire said.

"All sorts of stuff. Most of it didn't make a lot of sense. Nobody is capable of taking the long view these days. Be careful who you put your trust in. A bunch of crap like that. And after a couple glasses of wine, he made this

247

weird comment about being careful who you do business with. He sounded like my dad at one point."

Lance glanced at the bar where the bartender was smiling back at him.

"If you'll excuse me for a few minutes," he said, getting to his feet. "The bartender wants to talk surfing with me."

Josie and Chef Claire caught the look on his face and laughed.

"Sure, go right ahead," Chef Claire said.

"Happy hunting," Josie said.

"What?" Lance said, then his face reddened. "Oh, got it. Hey, you never know, right? I'll see you in a bit."

"Based on how she's been staring at him since I got here, I like his chances," Betty said, then took a sip.

"He'll be fine as long as he doesn't try to cook for her," Josie said.

"Indeed," Betty said, raising her glass in salute. "He's an interesting young man."

"We've been wondering if there's more to him than meets the eye," Josie said.

"Like what?" Betty said.

"It's hard to explain," Chef Claire said.

"Try me," Betty said, leaning forward.

"Well, given some of the things Bronwyn mentioned about Georgio, and since there's obviously something going on at the villa, we couldn't help but wonder if…"

"Wonder what?" Betty said, frowning.

"This is going to sound stupid," Chef Claire said.

"I promise not to laugh," Betty said.

"He's been spending a lot of time with Georgio," Chef Claire said. "And we started wondering if Lance might be working as an undercover agent for some government entity."

"You mean like the FBI?" Betty said.

"Yeah," Josie said. "It does sound kinda crazy, huh?"

"It's impossible," Betty said, shaking her head before taking a small sip of wine.

"Why do you say that?" Chef Claire said.

"Because I'm the undercover agent."

Chapter 22

Stunned, Josie reacted to Betty's news by gagging on a mouthful of wine and spraying it across the table. She coughed several times then wiped her mouth staring at Betty the entire time.

"Sorry," Josie said, tossing her napkin on the table.

"Smooth," Chef Claire said, wiping the table directly in front of her. She leaned back in her chair and studied Betty closely. "I didn't see that one coming."

"No kidding," Josie said, leaning forward in her seat. "You're with the FBI?"

"I am," Betty said softly as she looked back and forth at them. She took a small sip of wine. "Surprise."

"But you're…Canadian," Josie said.

"That's all you got?" Chef Claire said, laughing.

"Shut it," Josie said. "I'm still trying to recover from the news."

"Yes, I grew up in Canada," Betty said. "But I hold dual-citizenship. It comes in handy at times."

"Okay," Josie said, nodding. "Wow."

"Josie speechless," Chef Claire said. "Well done, Betty."

"Funny," Josie said, making a face at Chef Claire. "But I do have a couple of questions."

"Only a couple?" Betty said, then flashed a smile before taking another sip.

"You came here tonight to tell us?" Josie said.

"I did," Betty said. "We decided it was time."

"We? Agent Tompkins, right?" Chef Claire said.

"The one and only," Betty said. "We weren't planning on letting you in on our little secret, but after what happened to Emerson, Agent Tompkins wanted you to know."

"Because?" Chef Claire said.

"He's getting a little worried about your safety," Betty said with a shrug. "And he suggested I tell you, so you'll know who to come to if anything else happens while we're here."

"You think something else is going to happen?" Josie said.

Betty looked around the bar for several moments in silence then shrugged.

"Anything's possible," she said eventually.

"Well, that makes me feel so much better," Josie said.

"What the heck is going on around here?" Chef Claire said.

"I really can't divulge too much," Betty said. "Let's just say we're doing everything we can to shut down an operation of concern before it goes any further."

"An operation of concern?" Josie said, frowning. "Fed-speak for some really bad crap?"

Betty laughed then took another sip of her wine.

"Good one," she said. "Yes, some really bad crap is on the horizon."

"Georgio, right?" Chef Claire said.

"Yes. Among others."

"Please tell me Marco and Rosa aren't involved," Chef Claire said.

"Given the circumstances of their relationship with Georgio, I'm not sure yet."

"You're talking about the three million Georgio invested in their winery," Chef Claire said.

"Oh, you know about that, too?" Betty said, surprised.

"Marco told me," Chef Claire said.

"You two must be close," Betty said, casually swirling the wine in her glass.

Josie and Chef Claire made eye contact. Then Chef Claire focused on the FBI agent.

"Are you fishing, Betty?" Chef Claire said.

"No, just trying to protect you from ending up in a place you do not want to be."

"What do you want to know?" Chef Claire said.

"I think we know pretty much everything about your relationship with the Columbo couple," she said.

"Do you now?" Chef Claire said, her voice rising.

"Easy," Josie said, reaching out to place a hand on Chef Claire's forearm.

"You've been digging into my background?" Chef Claire said.

"It's what we do," Betty said as a simple statement of fact. "But don't worry, neither one of you are suspected of doing anything wrong."

"That makes me feel so much better," Chef Claire deadpanned.

"Relax. In an investigation like this, it shouldn't surprise you we're going to take a look at everyone."

"So, what did you find out about me?" Chef Claire said.

"You were a student when the Columbos were running their culinary school. After you graduated, you operated a food truck for a while, ended up working as the personal chef for a gentleman who is no longer with us. Then you decided to stay in Clay Bay and open the restaurant with Josie as one of your partners. Along with Suzy Chandler and her mother." Betty drained the rest of her wine then caught the bartender's eye and waved for another round of drinks. "And speaking for everyone within a hundred miles of Clay Bay, we thank you for doing that."

"Wait a sec," Josie said. "Were you working all those times you came to the restaurant?"

"Sometimes," Betty said. "Other times, I was off the clock."

"Does this have anything to do with somebody who's smuggling stuff across the River?" Chef Claire said.

"Agent Tompkins *was* chatty on the phone the other night," Betty said, then smiled at Chef Claire. "I'm not surprised. He's very fond of you."

"What else do you know about me?" Chef Claire said.

"Hang on," Josie said, holding a hand up to cut the conversation off. "Let's stick with the smuggling thing for a minute. What the heck is that all about?"

254

"It shouldn't surprise you people like to take advantage of the relative ease of going back and forth across the border by boat."

"Drugs?" Josie said.

"I really can't say," Betty said, shrugging it off.

"C'mon, Betty," Josie said. "Fess up. Somebody is moving large quantities of drugs in from Canada, aren't they?"

"I'm sure there are people trying to do that," Betty said.

"But it's not what you're investigating, is it?" Chef Claire said.

"In this particular case, no," she said softly.

"Well, if it isn't drugs, what is it?" Chef Claire said.

"I'd rather not say," Betty said.

"And I'd rather not have to eat Lance's food," Josie said. "But it's part of the program. C'mon, Betty. Who am I gonna tell?"

"If you know what's good for you, nobody."

"Is that some sort of threat?" Josie said.

"Not at all," Betty said. "It's just a dangerous situation that could get ugly in a hurry. And you don't want to get anywhere near it."

"Thanks for the tip," Josie said. "If it isn't drugs, what is it?"

They all looked up when the bartender arrived with their drinks. She set them down then headed back to the bar where Lance was sitting by himself. They all took small sips of wine then settled back into their chairs.

"So, what is it, Betty?" Josie said. "What the heck is going on back home?"

"We're dealing with a well-organized smuggling ring," Betty said. "Or at least we're trying to."

"But not drugs?" Josie said.

"No."

"Then what the heck is it?" Josie said, unwilling to let it go. "Booze? Wheat? Maple syrup?"

"No," Betty said, laughing. She glanced at Chef Claire. "She's not going to let it go, is she?"

"I don't like your chances," Chef Claire said.

"No, it's none of those things, Josie."

"Then what the heck are they smuggling across the border?"

"People."

"What?" Josie whispered.

"That's despicable," Chef Claire said.

256

"Yes, we think so too," Betty said. "And unless we're wrong about their intention to ramp up before winter arrives, you'll probably be seeing a lot of me in the near future."

"Unless we don't make it out of the villa alive," Josie said.

"I wouldn't worry," Betty said. "But if you do have concerns about your safety, be sure and let me know."

"You can count on it," Josie said, then shook her head. "Smuggling people. I can't believe it."

"You remember when we were in the car yesterday?" Chef Claire said.

"I do," Betty said. "What about it?"

"We were tossing out ideas about what Georgio and Emerson might be up to," Chef Claire said.

"I remember."

"So, you were just playing dumb the whole time?" Chef Claire said.

"Maybe a little," Betty said. "I still had some questions I needed answered."

"About us?" Josie said.

"No. But I was interested in hearing your ideas," Betty said. "I was impressed."

"Natalie," Chef Claire said.

"Yes, Natalie," Betty said. "The Bureau, along with several other of our intelligence agencies, have had her on the radar for a long time."

"And?" Chef Claire said.

"And despite her background, we don't think she's involved in this one."

"You're buying her story about being here just to see if she and Georgio might be able to reconnect?" Chef Claire said.

"I am," Betty said, then took a sip of wine and nodded in the general direction of the bar. "It looks like Lance has made a new friend."

"Apparently, the bartender wanted to talk surfing with him," Josie said.

"Even if she didn't, I'm sure he'd be talking about surfing," Betty said, laughing.

"What's his deal?" Josie said.

"What?"

"Well, if you've been checking into our backgrounds, you must have done the same thing with Lance."

"We did," Betty said. "Like he told us, he's a trust fund kid who's about to lose everything if he doesn't get his act together. Apparently, his parents aren't thrilled with his personal growth and development."

"Has he been on your radar?" Chef Claire said.

"No," Betty said. "We just started taking a look at him."

"Since the start of the week?" Josie said.

"Pretty much," Betty said with a shrug. Then she caught the look both women were giving her. "What is it?"

"I'm just wondering what it's like having access to everyone's personal information," Chef Claire said.

"To tell you the truth, it can be downright scary," Betty said softly. "And it's not my favorite part of the job."

"This is probably a dumb question," Josie said.

"Not a problem. I get them all the time," Betty said.

"Why don't you just arrest Georgio and get it over with?" she said. "It's pretty clear the guy is dirty."

"Oh, he's definitely as dirty as they come," Betty said. "But he's also one of the smartest people I've ever met."

"You haven't caught him in the act?" Chef Claire said.

"If we had, we wouldn't be having this conversation. But we're getting close."

259

"What exactly does the guy do?" Chef Claire said. "Bronwyn mentioned he was involved in arms dealing and some technology crap, but nothing specific."

"I doubt if Bronwyn knew any of the details," Betty said.

"Why's that?" Josie said.

"Because she would have told you," Betty said, shrugging. "Bronwyn Kingsley was known for two things. One was her undying love for herself. The other was her inability to keep her mouth shut."

"That's why she was killed?" Chef Claire said. "Because she talked to the wrong person?"

"We're not exactly sure why she was killed," Bronwyn said. "Or by whom. All we know for sure is how she was killed."

"The poison," Chef Claire said. "That's what this is all about, isn't it?"

"It's certainly high on the list," Betty said, glancing around the bar again to make sure they couldn't be overheard. "Georgio branched out into new ventures several years ago, and we're sure whatever substance killed her is one of his latest creations."

"So, it's like some sort of nerve gas?" Josie said. "Chemical warfare?"

"Yes. This is usually when the scary part of the job kicks in," Betty said. "I couldn't believe it when I got briefed about some of the stuff he has invented."

"I take it we're not talking about pasta makers," Josie said.

"Uh, no," Betty said, laughing. "But I have to give him credit. I love that machine."

"Why would Georgio bring the stuff with him this week?" Chef Claire said. "It's obviously dangerous to have around."

"A very good question," Betty said. "Either he needs to demonstrate to somebody how well it works, or he's trying to find someone to help him mass produce it. Maybe both."

"Emerson?" Chef Claire said.

"Not anymore," Betty said with a shrug.

"I thought his company manufactures stuff made out of metal and plastic," Josie said.

"It does. And unless we've completely missed something, Kingsley never did any chemical production."

"But he could have been working with Georgio to develop a way to transport or release the toxin, right?" Chef Claire said.

"Very good," Betty said, nodding. "That's exactly what we thought he was working with Georgio on. But we have no idea what they were trying to come up with."

"It's going to be a bit hard to do now," Josie said. "Now that Emerson and Bronwyn are both dead."

"It certainly won't make it any easier," Betty said. "All we know for sure is the toxin works as advertised. We've never seen anything like it."

"Is Commissario Bruno in the loop?" Josie said.

"Absolutely not," Betty said, shaking her head. "And he's not going to be."

"Somebody comes to Italy, possibly an American, and kills two people with some exotic poison? Don't you think that's something the Italian government would want to know about?"

"Absolutely," Betty said. "And at some point, they'll be brought in. But it will be done at a much higher level than Commissario Bruno." She glanced back and forth at them. "Do you understand what I'm saying?"

"Got it," Chef Claire said.

"Mum's the word," Josie said.

"Fortunately, it was two Americans who died," Betty said, then flushed red with embarrassment. "I'm sorry. That came out wrong. Wow, this job is really starting to affect the way I see the world. What I meant to say was, if either of the victims had been Italian, we'd be having a different conversation with the local authorities."

"Who do you think killed them?" Chef Claire said.

"When it comes to Bronwyn, we're still baffled," Betty said. "Emerson's death appears a bit clearer."

"The black SUV that passed us yesterday," Chef Claire said. "It turned off on the road that led to the golf course."

"It did," Betty said.

"But you don't know who it was, right?" Josie said.

"All we know is the vehicle wasn't one of ours."

"Who the heck do you think it was?" Josie said.

"I don't know," Betty said. "Maybe another government wanting to get their hands on whatever the stuff is. One of Kingsley's competitors who somehow knew what he was working on and wanted to take him out and cut a deal for themselves. A terrorist organization. Pharmaceutical company. Take your pick."

"Pharmaceutical company?" Josie said, raising an eyebrow. "Another one of those scary things you were talking about?"

"You don't want to know," Betty said. "And even if you did, I couldn't tell you."

"The next time you're thinking about going to cooking school to catch up with old friends, remind me to hit you with your bat," Josie said to Chef Claire.

"No argument from me," Chef Claire said, shaking her head. "This is the sort of stuff you deal with on a regular basis?"

"It is. It's hard work, sometimes depressing, and often leaves me baffled about the state of the human condition. But I still love it. And when you boil it all down, I suppose there are worse ways to make a living," Betty said.

"Name two," Josie deadpanned, then grinned.

"Mortician and Port-A-Potty cleaner," Betty said without hesitation. "I've got a whole list. Should I go on?"

"No," Josie said, laughing. "I take your point."

"So, what do we do?" Chef Claire said.

"You don't do anything," Betty said. "The only reason we had this conversation was because Agent Tompkins

264

wanted you to know. Like I said, he's a bit concerned about your safety."

"Aren't you?" Josie said.

"Not yet," Betty said. "But I'll let you know if anything changes."

"Do you think Marco and Rosa are involved in any of this?" Chef Claire said.

"Probably only to the extent Georgio is going to need his three million back," Betty said.

"Marco said he was looking for another investor because Rosa isn't comfortable having Georgio as a partner," Chef Claire said.

"I'm sure she's not," Betty said. "And things are getting worse for Georgio."

"Georgio is also having money problems?" Chef Claire said.

"They're just starting," Betty said, unable to hide her grin.

"What are you guys up to?" Josie said.

"You're messing with his bank accounts, aren't you?" Chef Claire said.

"I can't talk about it," Betty said. "Let's just say Georgio will soon be looking for ways to get his hands on some cash in a hurry."

"You set all this up for the week, didn't you?" Chef Claire said.

"Again, I can't talk about it. But I can say we definitely wanted to take advantage of the fact Georgio and Emerson were both going to be here for the week."

"What are you going to do now that Emerson is dead?" Josie said.

"My job."

"Well, I kinda figured," Josie said, shaking her head.

"I'm going to keep my eyes and ears open, see what I can figure out, and take whatever action seems most appropriate," Betty said.

"And try not to get scared in the process?" Josie said.

"You're a quick study," Betty said, raising her glass in salute. "I think we should have one more glass of wine. Drinks are on Uncle Sam tonight."

"It's the least he can do," Josie said, tossing back what was left in her glass.

"No," Betty said, shaking her head. "Trust me, he can do a lot less."

Chapter 23

Marco was halfway through his introductory lesson on Italian soups and stews when Josie leaned over and whispered to Chef Claire.

"He's just going through the motions."

"Yeah, he's totally distracted," Chef Claire whispered back. "I guess we can't blame him, huh?"

Josie slowly nodded and refocused on Marco's presentation. A few minutes, he placed the large knife he was using to demonstrate different ways to slice and dice a wide variety of vegetables on the kitchen island. He looked around the class then forced a sad smile.

"I'm sorry," Marco said. "If I was sitting through this lesson, I'm sure I'd find all of it incredibly basic and boring."

"No, it's good stuff," Betty said. "You make it look so easy."

"Thanks, Betty," Marco said, laughing. "Fortunately for all of you, I'm done talking." He removed a small stack of index cards from his shirt pocket and casually flipped through them. "Rosa and I thought we'd do something a bit different today. You'll all be assigned a different dish. A lot of the prep techniques will be the same, but we didn't think anybody would want to eat a half dozen versions of the same dish for lunch."

"Lunch?" Lance said. "We're not cooking for dinner?"

"No," Marco said. "Part of today's lesson is to demonstrate you don't need to slave over a stove all day to make great Italian food."

"So, what are making this afternoon?" Lance said.

"We'll be doing a fridge clean," Marco said. "You'll be making a dish of your choice from whatever leftovers you find. We'll mix those dishes in tonight with a few of the soups and stews you make this morning. In your course materials, you'll find a whole list of recipes to choose from. And Rosa and I will be working with you on an individual basis and answering any questions you might have."

"Leftovers," Chef Claire whispered as she leaned in close to Josie. "Probably somewhat of a foreign concept to you, huh?"

"Funny."

He passed the index cards out and waited until everyone had a chance to review their assigned dish.

"You'll find all the ingredients you need in the fridge and pantry," Marco said. "We'll be eating lunch around one so keep that in mind as you're working on your dish. We'll put some snacks out around ten, but feel free to take breaks whenever you like." He glanced around again waiting to see if there were questions. "Okay, let's get started. Have fun."

"What did you get?" Chef Claire said, glancing at Josie's card.

"Italian wedding soup," Josie said. "One of my favorites. It looks pretty easy."

"You should get started," Chef Claire said.

"The recipe says it only takes an hour," Josie said. "What's the hurry?"

"Read the recipe again."

"Crap. It's only an hour after the chicken stock is made," Josie said, frowning. "I suppose I should make a stock from scratch, right?"

"It's your call," Chef Claire deadpanned. "But I don't think you needed to fly to Italy to learn how to open a can."

"Yeah. Good point."

Marco, standing nearby, laughed and pointed at one of the refrigerators.

"You'll find lots of carcass bones in the fridge," he said.

"Why is my card blank, Marco?" Chef Claire said.

"I thought you might want to work with me making bread," Marco said. "I searched high and low for something to challenge you, but couldn't come up with anything."

"Yeah, I've got that one covered. Given the climate back home, we serve a lot of soups and stews at the restaurant," Chef Claire said. "But my bread needs work."

"Then you've come to the right place," Marco said, laughing. "When are you making your dough?"

"Early in the morning," Chef Claire said. "It rises for about four hours."

"That's one of your problems," Marco said, pointing to a large lump on the counter covered by a towel. "Try making your dough the day before and letting it rise overnight."

"How long do you let your dough go?"

"Twelve hours minimum," Marco said.

"Really?" Chef Claire said. "I never realized it took so much time."

"It doesn't," Marco said. "And you can certainly make great bread a lot faster. But you said you wanted to make *world-class* rustic bread."

"Lead the way," Chef Claire said, laughing as she spread her arms wide.

"I'll show you how to start the dough in a minute," Marco said, heading for the counter. He returned carrying the toweled object and set it down in front of them. He pulled the towel back like a magician performing a reveal. "But first, let's get this one going on its second rise."

"It's beautiful," Chef Claire said, gently probing the dough with her fingers. "How long does it need?"

"An hour or two," Marco said. "It should rise noticeably. You'll know it when you see it."

"Got it," Chef Claire said.

"Here's the next tip," he said. "Don't knead it. Gently fold it into a ball. Like this."

Chef Claire watched as he assembled the dough into shape.

"Be gentle," he said. "I call it the lover's touch."

"If you say so," Chef Claire said, laughing.

"I've meant to ask. How are things going on the personal front?"

271

"I think I'm in a slump," Chef Claire said.

"I find that hard to believe," Marco said. "You've just been spending too much time at work."

"There's no doubt about it, Marco."

"Hang in there. It's going to happen for you."

"Thanks, Marco. How are you holding up?"

"I'm afraid it's going to take a lot more than a great loaf of bread to solve our problems," he said, setting the dough aside and wiping his hands on a dish towel. "I need to make the rounds and check in on everybody. I'll meet you back here in about twenty minutes."

"Okay," Chef Claire said. "I better go check in on Josie to see what sort of mess she's making."

"I've been watching her the past few days," Marco said. "She's a good cook."

"She is," Chef Claire said. "Just not a tidy one."

"Yes, I noticed," he said, laughing.

Chef Claire headed for Josie who was using tongs to maneuver a chicken carcass and assorted vegetables in a large pot.

"Smells great," Chef Claire said.

"Are you sure this is right?" Josie said, glancing over her shoulder. "The pot is snapping at me."

272

"You want it on high heat for a few more minutes," Chef Claire said, peering down into the pot. "It needs a bit more color. Just keep stirring it around."

"If you say so," Josie said, working the tongs through the pot. "I just hope Marco doesn't mind me filling up his kitchen with smoke."

"You're cooking," Chef Claire said. "If you don't get some smoke, you ain't trying."

"Well, thank you, Ms. Childs," she said, pushing her hair back from her face. "What are you making?"

"Bread."

"Slacker," Josie deadpanned. "How's Marco doing?"

"Not well."

"Do you think we should tell him about Betty?"

"No," Chef Claire said. "I think she should tell him."

"And if she refuses?" Josie said, glancing over her shoulder.

"I would take it as a clue Marco is also a target of the investigation."

"Great minds think alike," Josie said.

"Okay, that's good," Chef Claire said, taking another look into the pot. "Lower the heat and cover it with water. It needs to simmer for at least an hour."

"Got it," Josie said. "I'll get started on the rest of the prep work for the soup."

"You've got plenty of time," Chef Claire said. "I thought we'd give Suzy a call."

"Good idea," Josie said, sliding the lid over the pot. She wiped her hands then gestured toward the door. "The veranda awaits."

They headed for the patio doors and were buffeted by a stiff breeze as soon as they stepped outside. Chef Claire glanced around then pointed at an area protected from the wind. They sat down, and Josie made the call and set the phone on the armrest.

"This is Suzy."

"Hey, it's us," Josie said.

"Sorry, I didn't even check the number," Suzy said. "How's it going?"

"It's good," Josie said. "We're making soups and stews today."

"Yum. I was thinking about making something like that as well. It's cold here today."

"How are the dogs?" Chef Claire said.

"They're great," Suzy said. "And they still haven't mentioned disowning you guys."

274

"Give Captain a big hug for me."

"Ditto," Chef Claire said.

"Will do. How's the other situation going?"

"I think the best word to describe it is *developing*," Josie said.

"Developing how?" Suzy said, immediately concerned.

"Don't worry, we're fine," Josie said. "But it's a weird situation that got a lot weirder last night."

"Really? Okay, this I gotta hear."

"We found out who the undercover agent is," Chef Claire said.

"The surfer dude?"

"No, it's Betty," Josie said.

"Betty from Ottawa?"

"Yeah," Josie said.

"How the heck did you figure it out?"

"She told us," Chef Claire said.

"What? Why would she…hang on," Suzy said, her concern rapidly ratcheting. "Agent Tompkins told her to tell you, didn't he?"

"How the heck did you know?" Josie said, glancing at Chef Claire.

"He's worried about your safety, isn't he?"

275

"We're fine," Chef Claire said. "Betty said they wanted us to know just in case."

"Just in case what?"

"Relax, Suzy," Josie said. "Think of it as an insurance policy. We're totally safe."

"My advice is to have a bowl of soup and then get the heck out of there," Suzy said.

"The school ends tomorrow," Chef Claire said. "And we're getting on the road as soon as it does."

"Okay. But stick close to Betty tonight," Suzy said, then paused before continuing. "Is she working from the idea this guy Georgio is behind all of this?"

"I don't think she's looking at him for the murders, but he's definitely in her sights as the catalyst," Chef Claire said. "There's no doubt he's dirty."

"Stay out of his way," Suzy said. "What about Natalie?"

"She seems to be telling the truth about why she's here," Josie said.

"Trying to rekindle the relationship with good food and wine?" Suzy said.

"Yeah," Josie said. "We don't think she's involved in any of this."

"I still find it hard to believe," Suzy said. "Have you seen her this morning?"

"Of course," Chef Claire said. "Counting us, we're down to eight students."

"What's she doing?"

"She's making Pasta e Fagioli," Chef Claire said.

"And she's not acting strange?"

"We're talking about Natalie here, Suzy," Josie said. "Of course, she's acting strange."

"You know what I mean. What about Betty? How does she seem today?"

"The same as she always does," Josie said. "But I imagine it's how they're trained."

"I wish I were there," Suzy said.

"I'm sure you do," Josie said, laughing. "But your instructions are to take it easy and get your rest. By the way, how are you doing?"

"I'm getting fat," Suzy said. "How do you think I'm doing?"

"There seems to be a lot of that going around," Chef Claire deadpanned.

"Shut it."

"What?" Suzy said.

"Chef Claire is being a pain," Josie said.

"She's put on five pounds since we've been here," Chef Claire said.

"Why don't you say it a little louder?" Josie said. "I don't think the Swiss could hear you."

"Really?" Suzy said, then laughed. "Oh, my. How the mighty have fallen. It's about time."

"No kidding," Chef Claire said.

"New topic, please," Josie snapped.

"We need to get back to class," Chef Claire said.

"Yeah, I need to get going, too. My mom's making breakfast."

"Give her a hug from us," Chef Claire said.

"Will do. And make sure you give me an update if anything else happens."

"You got it," Chef Claire said.

"And Josie?"

"What?"

"Try not to eat too much."

"Hey, I'm not the only one in the house getting fat."

"No, but at least I have a good excuse."

Chapter 24

Josie and Chef Claire both nodded when the server offered the next bowl of soup. They ate a spoonful and swallowed in tandem. Josie slowly reached for her napkin and wiped her mouth before taking a long sip of water. She again covered her mouth with the napkin and snuck a quick look at Chef Claire.

"Oh, my God," Josie whispered. "What do we do now?"

"We eat just enough not to hurt his feelings," Chef Claire said, swallowing hard.

"Use your napkin."

"Did I spill?"

"No, but the napkin will hide the look on your face."

"It's so salty," Chef Claire said, slowly wiping her mouth.

"A salt lick is salty," Josie whispered, then had a thought. "This must be the stuff salt licks are made from."

"Maybe he developed a taste for it over the years," Chef Claire said, staring down at the steaming bowl.

"What?"

"From spending all that time in the ocean."

"Funny," Josie said, tentatively dipping her spoon in the soup.

"How do you like it?" Lance said, glancing across the table.

"It's quite unique, Lance," Chef Claire said, forcing down another spoonful.

"Gee, thanks, Chef Claire," Lance said, grinning at her. "It means a lot coming from you."

"Minestrone, right?"

"Yeah," he said, nodding. "At least my version of it."

"I'm getting a hint of salami," Chef Claire said.

"A hint?" Josie whispered. "We must have a different definition."

"Shut it," Chef Claire said, again wiping her mouth. "Salami. Interesting choice."

"It's not too salty is it?"

"It's delicious," Georgio said as he rapidly worked his way through his bowl.

Chef Claire, puzzled, glanced at Josie.

"Probably not a word I would use," Josie whispered.

"What the heck is he talking about?"

"He must be sucking up, right?"

"And he doesn't want to say or do anything to blow whatever deal they're working on," Chef Claire said, nodding. "Yeah, I can make that work."

A loud knock on the front door caused everyone to stop eating momentarily.

"I'll get it," Marco said, getting up from his chair.

Moments later, he returned trailed by Commissario Bruno. The detective glanced around the table and nodded his approval at the collection of serving bowls.

"Everything looks fantastic," Commissario Bruno said. "It must be soup night. I love soup."

"Have a seat," Marco said. "We have plenty."

"No, I can't stay, thanks."

"Oh, you must try the minestrone, Commissario," Josie said.

She grabbed a clean spoon and placed it in her bowl then held it out to him. He gave it some thought then nodded and accepted the bowl.

"I can't believe you did that," Chef Claire whispered.

"You're just pissed because I thought of it first."

They watched as he took a sip, flinched, then quickly recovered. He forced down another spoonful then set the bowl on the table and wiped his mouth before reaching for the glass of water Rosa was holding out.

"Just like your mama used to make, huh?" Josie said with a grin.

"Sure, let's go with that," he said, giving Josie a sideways glance before turning all business. "I just stopped by to let you know you're all free to go."

"Have you found the murderer?" Betty said.

"No, we haven't," Commissario Bruno said. "And I have to say, I don't like our chances. But since we have no reason to keep you here, feel free to leave whenever you're ready."

"Have you figured out what killed them?" Betty said.

"No, our lab is still working on it," he said, subconsciously glancing at the bowl of minestrone. "Since we don't have a clue what we're dealing with, we are proceeding very cautiously."

"Just so you don't end up killing one of your techs in the process?" Betty said.

"Something like that," the detective said. "If anything changes, or if I need to speak with any of you, I'll be in touch."

"Thanks for all your hard work, Commissario," Marco said.

"I'm afraid I didn't do much," he said, then took another look around. "It was nice meeting all of you. Try to enjoy the rest of your dinner."

"Take good care of Rico," Josie said.

"Oh, I will," he said, beaming. "He's waiting for me in the car. I should get going. Take care and travel safely."

He waved then headed for the door. Moments later, the sound of his car heading down the driveway could be heard. A server arrived carrying a large bowl and began serving.

"What's the next course, Enrico?"

"It's the wedding soup, sir."

"Wonderful. Josie's dish," Marco said, focusing on her. "Would you like to describe your dish before or after we try it?"

"Oh, let's do it after," Josie said, then muttered under her breath. "I gotta this taste out of my mouth."

Chef Claire stifled a snort then sampled the soup and nodded her approval.

"Well done."

"Thanks," Josie said. "You were right. Making the stock from scratch makes all the difference."

"So, Georgio," Rosa said, not looking up from her bowl of soup. "Now that the police have removed the travel ban, where are you headed next?"

"If I didn't know better, Rosa," Georgio said, flashing her a crocodile smile. "I'd swear you were trying to get rid of me."

"Relax, Georgio," Marco said, laughing nervously. "She's not saying any such thing. Isn't that right, dear?"

"What?" Rosa said, glancing at her husband.

"I'm sure you agree," Marco said, forcing a smile.

"I do," she said, briefly glaring at Georgio before refocusing on her bowl. "Chef Claire's right. The wedding soup is excellent."

"Please, Rosa," Marco said. "Not tonight."

"All I asked was where he was headed next," she said softly. "It's not that hard of a question."

"Rosa," Marco whispered. "Let's not do this here."

"It's okay, Marco," Georgio said as he reached for his wine glass. "If you must know, Rosa, Lance has invited me to California. We're going to partner up on a new venture.

284

And he's going to teach me how to surf. It's something I've always wanted to learn."

"Surfing with the sharks, huh?" Rosa said with a big grin. "You should feel right at home."

"Here we go," Josie whispered.

"Yeah," Chef Claire whispered back. "Stay on your toes. Betty said she was thinking about pushing the conversation tonight. This might be her best chance."

"You'll have to excuse my wife, Georgio," Marco said. "I think she may have had a bit too much wine."

"I haven't had nearly enough," Rosa said, reaching for a bottle sitting nearby.

"Whereabouts in California do you live, Lance?" Betty said.

"Near San Diego," he said with a shrug. "But I go up and down the coast as needed."

"Wherever the waves take you, right?" Betty said.

"Exactly," Lance said, raising his glass in salute.

Betty returned the salute then took a sip before focusing on Georgio.

"Why surfing?"

"I like the idea of a man alone against the elements," Georgio said, going for philosophical.

"Conquering Mother Nature, right?" Betty said, her smile now permanent.

"Yeah, I guess you could say that," Georgio said, nodding. "And she certainly does need to be tamed from time to time."

"Good luck with that," Josie said.

"I'm sorry. But I'm not following," Georgio said, glancing at her.

"Trying to tame Mother Nature," Josie said.

"You don't agree with the concept?" he said.

"Actually, I think it's an exercise in futility," Josie said.

"Interesting. How so?" Georgio said.

"A couple of things," Josie said, swirling the wine in her glass. "We live in an area where Mother Nature's power is on full display during the winter months."

"You got that right," Betty said, nodding. "Cold, wind, snow, ice. Oh, Canada."

"You gonna start singing your national anthem?" Georgio said, then laughed.

"I don't sing," Betty said, her smile fading.

"But the main reason I think it's futile is because you can't beat Mother Nature. We're barely able to play her to a tie at the moment," Josie said.

"Awkward sports metaphors aside, why do you say that?" Georgio said, placing his elbows on the table and leaning forward.

"Because when she's good and ready, and we've finally ticked her off to the point where she decides to do something about it, Mother Nature will shake us off faster than our dogs can get rid of a flea," Chef Claire said.

"What she said," Josie said, nodding at Chef Claire before taking another sip of wine.

"Are you saying you're not concerned about the future of the planet?" Lance said.

"I'm not saying that at all," Josie said. "Quite the opposite. I was merely pointing out the futility of trying to control the natural order by constantly doing stupid stuff that only makes things worse."

"Are you referring to the political dimensions of the world's problems?" Georgio said.

"They're certainly part of it," Josie said.

"But not nearly all," Chef Claire said.

"Yeah, we can't forget corporate greed and corruption," Josie said.

"So, I take it you two are lefties," Georgio said.

"No, we're both righthanded," Josie deadpanned.

Everyone laughed, breaking the tension at the table. But it quickly returned, and Georgio fixed a hard stare on Josie.

"So, what's your solution?" he said.

"Well, the people who ultimately run the place could stop doing stupid crap around the planet," Josie said. "Maybe if people had a chance to catch their breath for a while, things might start to improve."

"Nah," Georgio said, shaking his head. "It's not gonna happen. Besides, it wouldn't work."

"Why's that?" Betty said.

"Because there are simply too many people," Georgio said, sitting back and spreading his hands apart to emphasize his point. "There will never be enough resources to go around to handle the billions who live here."

"But you're working on that, right, Georgio?" Rosa said, tossing back the rest of her wine before refilling her glass.

288

"Try to control your wife, Marco," Georgio said, not even bothering to glance down the table. He glanced across the table at all three women before finally fixing another hard stare on Josie. "So, your solution is to let *Mother Nature* do her thing and see what happens?"

"Not at all," Josie said, shaking her head. "All I'm saying is we might want to try working with her once in a while."

"I see," Georgio said, chuckling. "Because if we don't, mankind is somehow doomed?"

"Doomed is such a harsh term," Josie said. "But I will say, if the people who run the place don't start making some changes pretty soon, I don't like our chances."

"We'll all be long gone before it's a real problem," Georgio said, waving it off. "Let future generations worry about it."

"I'd like to make a toast," Rosa said, raising her glass.

"Please, don't," Marco whispered.

"To Georgio and his merry band of men. May short-term, self-interest continue to rule the day," Rosa said, glaring down the table. "Join me in toast and raise your glasses. To the Bottom- Feeders. May Mother Nature take you first. And may her justice be swift...and painful."

289

"Okay, I think I've had enough for one week," Georgio said, sliding his chair back and standing. "You know, Lance, I think there's a late flight tonight out of Milan we can still catch. I don't see why we shouldn't head out now."

"Sure. Works for me," Lance said, getting up. "I just need to pack. I'll be back in five."

"My stuff is already in the car," Georgio said, then addressed the group. "It was wonderful meeting all of you, and I hope you enjoy the pasta maker. Don't forget to tell all your friends."

"Oh, don't leave, Georgio," Rosa said, taunting the inventor. "It was just getting good. I was so hoping you'd regale us with your tales from around the globe dealing with the indigent indigenous."

"Try saying that three times fast," Josie whispered to Chef Claire.

"Yeah, it was a good shot," Chef Claire whispered back.

"But before I go," Georgio said, reaching for his phone. "I'd like to get a group picture."

"Why?" Rosa said.

"For the memory," he said with a shrug. "Despite the rather unpleasant nature of tonight's conversation, I've had a wonderful time this week." He glanced around the room and pointed. "Let's do it in front of the fireplace."

Everyone looked at each other, shrugged, then assembled in front of the mantel. Georgio glanced around, phone in hand, and began gesturing.

"Let's have our hosts front and center," he said. "Marco and Rosa. If you'd be kind enough to kneel down right there. Perfect. And let's have everyone huddle around them and lean in close. Closer."

"This is weird," Josie said.

"I hate posing for pictures," Chef Claire said.

Seconds later, she visibly flinched.

"Don't do that," Josie snapped. "You're worse than Suzy."

"Please hold steady, Chef Claire," Georgio said.

"Hang on a sec," Chef Claire said, giving Josie a wide-eyed stare. "I've got a foot cramp."

"Are you okay?" Betty said, from her position to the right of Josie.

"I'll be fine in a minute," Chef Claire said, squeezing Josie's arm hard.

"Ow. What the heck is the matter with you?"

"I just told you," Chef Claire whispered. "I hate *posing* for pictures."

"Since when?"

"Since we got *here*."

"Here? You started to hate getting your picture taken when you got here?" Josie said, baffled.

"Not taken. *Posing*," Chef Claire said through clenched teeth.

Josie frowned. Then her eyes went wide.

"Holy crap," Josie said, then looked at Georgio. "What's your hurry, Georgio? Shouldn't we wait until Lance gets back?"

"It won't be necessary," Georgio said, examining his phone. "I'll be seeing lots of Lance." He took another look at the group and shook his head. "Chef Claire, I need you to move in even closer."

"You got it, Georgio," Chef Claire said, reaching behind her back.

"What are you doing?" Josie whispered.

"Just follow my lead."

"Don't do anything stupid," Josie said.

"Like stand here and get my picture taken?"

"Fair point."

292

Georgio knelt down in front of them about five feet away and raised the phone to his eyes. He was about to take the picture when the fireplace poker hit him hard on the elbow. The phone flew across the floor, and Georgio dropped face down on the floor screaming in agony.

"Nice shot," Josie said, watching as Chef Claire stood directly over the writhing Georgio.

"Thanks," Chef Claire said.

"What the heck did you do that for?" Marco said, leaning down to check on the condition of Georgio.

"You'll see," Chef Claire said, still holding the poker. She quickly glanced around at everyone. "Don't touch that phone."

"The phone," Betty whispered. "Well, I'll be damned."

"Yeah, it's definitely the phone," Chef Claire said.

"What is going on, Donato?" Maria Peccati said in halting English.

"Non ne ho idea," her husband responded in Italian.

Georgio rolled over onto his back grasping his arm. He glared up Chef Claire who continued to stand directly over him brandishing the poker.

"What the hell is wrong with you?" he said, starting to push himself upright with his good arm.

293

"You want another one?" Chef Claire said, raising the poker.

"No, I think I'll pass," he said, sitting down. "Marco, hand me my phone. I need to call my lawyer."

"Don't touch the phone," Betty said, reaching behind her back and removing a pair of handcuffs.

"What do you think you're doing?" Georgio said, staring at her in disbelief.

"Arresting you," Betty said, handcuffing him. "I'm gonna cut you a break and leave your hands cuffed in front of you. I don't think I'll be able to bend your arm behind your back."

"Betty?" Marco said softly. "What are you doing?"

"I just told you, Marco," she said, flashing her badge at him. "I'm arresting him. FBI."

"FBI?" Maria Peccati said, staring in disbelief at her husband who could only shrug back with a wide-eyed stare.

"You're with the FBI?" Rosa said.

"I am," Betty said, staring down at Georgio. "You were so close. I can't believe I never made the connection." She turned to Chef Claire. "When did you figure it out?"

"When he was getting ready to take the picture," Chef Claire said. "I was telling Josie how much I hated posing for pictures and it just came to me."

"What came to you?" Marco said.

"How Bronwyn and Emerson died," Chef Claire said.

"I think I'd like to hear this," Rosa said, sitting down on the couch.

"Me too," Marco said, taking a seat next to her.

"Whatever toxin that killed both of them is stored inside Georgio's phone," Chef Claire said. "And the protective case, another of Georgio's latest inventions, does a lot more than keep the phone from being damaged."

"It does?" Marco said, glancing down at the phone.

"It also functions as a storage and distribution system for the toxin," Chef Claire said. "It must have some sort of sprayer. You know, like an aerosol can."

"Preposterous," Georgio said with a snort. "Don't be ridiculous. It's just a phone."

"Then I take it you wouldn't mind if I tested it out on you?" Betty said, smiling at him.

"Never mind," Georgio said, then stared down at the floor. "Forget I even mentioned it."

"So, if he had taken the photo, there's a chance we would have all been killed?" Rosa said.

"I'm gonna go with a hundred percent," Chef Claire said.

"You scumbag," Marco said, glaring at Georgio who continued to massage his arm.

"You're the one who couldn't get her to shut up," Georgio said, glaring at Rosa. "And I offer you an extra two million, and she laughs in my face?"

"We don't need your money," Rosa said.

"Hah," Georgio said. "Without my money, you're gonna need a miracle."

"Enough," Marco said, then frowned. "You're saying he killed Bronwyn and Emerson?"

"I'm almost positive he killed Emerson," Betty said. "But he didn't kill Bronwyn."

"Then who did?" Marco said.

"She did it to herself," Chef Claire said.

"Suicide?" Rosa said, stunned.

"No, it was an accident," Chef Claire said. "Remember when she was talking at dinner that night about how her marriage was on the rocks?"

"I do," Marco said. "And she also said she and Georgio were thinking about getting back together. But how does it fit in with her death?"

"Georgio asked her to send him a message as soon as she made her mind up about wanting to give their relationship another shot," Chef Claire said. "When we found her body, her blouse was partially undone, and she was wearing bright red lipstick."

"And she was all puckered up like she was about to give someone a kiss," Betty said.

"That was the message," Chef Claire said. "Bronwyn was going to send Georgio a sexy photo for him to find on his phone later."

"So, she took the picture and sprayed herself with poison?" Rosa said.

"Death by selfie," Josie deadpanned.

"Ironic, huh?" Chef Claire said.

"Retribution for the truly self-absorbed," Josie said.

"There's no need to be cruel," Georgio said. "Bronwyn was a wonderful woman."

"And you knew what had happened as soon as you saw her sprawled out on the floor," Betty said.

"Yes," Georgio whispered. "I did."

"And the first thing you did was grab your phone off the table," Betty said.

"That's right," Josie said. "I remember. I couldn't help but notice how different the phone looked from mine." She glanced down at Georgio. "I asked you about it the next day, and you told me it had a specially designed cover you developed."

"It was the truth," Georgio said.

"Just a bit incomplete, right?"

He shrugged and went back to massaging his arm.

"What about Emerson?" Rosa said.

"It had to be Georgio," Chef Claire said. "Somehow he managed to get away from Lance for a while when they were in town."

"It's definitely a possibility," Betty said, reaching for her purse. "Or Lance is working with him."

"So, what was the deal, Georgio?" Chef Claire said. "You were driving the black SUV that passed us. Then you made the turn into the golf course."

Georgio remained silent.

"You must have grabbed a golf cart and drove around until you spotted Emerson on the twelfth green," Chef

298

Claire said. "What did you do? Talk him into posing for a picture? The view of the lake must have been fantastic."

Georgio merely shrugged.

"It's okay, Georgio. Don't talk," Betty said, pulling a handgun from her purse. "As soon as this new toxin gets identified, a murder charge is going to be the least of your problems." She tossed her purse on the table. "Now, all we need to do is figure out how Lance is involved."

"Figure out how Lance is involved in what?" the surfer said, strolling into the dining room with a travel bag draped over his shoulder. "What the heck is going on?"

"Come on in and have a seat, Lance," Betty said, extending her arm toward him.

"You're pointing a gun at me?"

"Nothing gets past him, huh?" Josie said, glancing at Chef Claire.

"Don't start."

"Just sit quietly for a minute, Lance," Betty said, flashing her credentials at him. "I have a few questions for you."

"FBI?" Lance said with a frown.

"Yes, I am."

Lance started laughing and didn't stop for a long time.

299

"Okay, I'll play," Betty said. "What on earth is so funny?"

"I need to show you something," Lance said, reaching inside his coat pocket. He stopped when he heard Betty rack a shell into the chamber.

"Don't do anything stupid, Lance," Betty said, staring hard at the surfer.

"Relax, Betty," he said. "My gun is packed in my bag. You know, since I didn't think I was going to need it tonight."

"His gun?" Josie said.

Chef Claire shrugged without taking her eyes off the action in front of her.

"I'm going to do this very slowly, Betty," Lance said.

"Good choice on your part," she said.

"Okay, here we go," he said, removing an object from his pocket. "You're FBI, huh?"

"Yes."

"Well, then, I'm going to see your FBI and raise you a CIA," he said, holding out his credentials.

"What?" Betty whispered, stunned.

"Yeah," Lance said, handing it to her to examine. "Small world, huh?"

"CIA?" Georgio whispered, then rubbed his forehead with his good arm. "Are you kidding me? I'm such an idiot."

"I don't believe it," Betty said, studying Lance's credentials before handing them back. "What's the CIA doing here?"

"Obviously, the same thing you are."

"Unbelievable," Josie said.

"Yeah, intra-governmental coordination at its finest," Chef Claire said, then focused on the two Feds. "Don't you people ever talk to each other?"

"This is embarrassing," Betty said.

"Yeah, a little bit," Lance said with a shrug. "But it's certainly not the first time it's happened. Okay, Betty, great work. I'll take it from here."

"Like hell you will," Betty said. "This is my collar."

"No, this is international," Lance said. "I don't want to argue territorial rights here. But this situation is right in our strike zone. It's what the Agency deals with around the planet on a daily basis."

"Nice try, Lance," Betty said. "The FBI has over sixty overseas field offices working in well over a hundred countries."

"A hundred and eighty, actually," Lance said. "But who's counting, huh?"

"No way you're taking this one from me."

"I'm the one who convinced him to cut Emerson loose and go with me on the deal," Lance said.

"So?" Betty said, scowling at Lance. "I'm the one who got her hands on the stuff." Then she glanced at Chef Claire. "With a lot of help."

"You had him kill Emerson?" Marco said.

"No, he came up with it on his own," Lance said. "Didn't you, Georgio? I guess you didn't want him hanging around in case he started talking to the wrong people." He focused on the FBI agent. "I'm sorry, but you're gonna have to walk away, Betty."

"Not a chance."

"Then I guess we've reached an impasse," Lance said, sitting back in his chair and draping a leg over his knee. "Tell you what. Let's share it."

Betty gave it some serious thought then nodded.

"That might work. This case is certainly big enough for both of us to get plenty of kudos."

"And we can present it to the public as an example of how two great organizations worked together to bring down a black-market arms dealer," he said.

"Oh, I love it," Betty said, tossing her gun back into her purse. "A man and a woman working seamlessly together. Some great optics for both organizations."

"Yeah, and I think there might be a couple of other ways we can juice the story," Lance said.

"I'd love to hear your ideas," Betty said. "Maybe after we take care of Inspector Psycho over there, we can sit down for a drink and discuss it. Or grab some dinner."

"Perfect," Lance said, getting to his feet. "You want to make your call first?"

"I would," Betty said. "Such a gentleman. Hard to find these days."

"I try," he said, flashing a big smile.

"Do you believe this?" Josie said.

"What are you gonna do," Chef Claire said, shaking her head.

"I'm getting a toothache," Josie said, then caught the look the two agents were now sharing. "Hey, get a room."

They both flushed with embarrassment and Betty made a quick call. She hung up and nodded at Lance.

"Okay, your turn."

"Cool," he said, patting his pockets. "Now, what the heck did I do with my phone?"

"Whatever you do," Chef Claire said. "Don't use the one on the floor."

"What?" Lance said, confused.

"I'll fill you in later," Betty said. "Here, use mine."

"Thanks, Betty."

He made a quick call then handed the phone back.

"Now, we wait," he said, sitting back down. "My guys said they wouldn't be long."

"I'm sure they won't," Betty said, laughing. "As soon as you told your folks the FBI was here, they probably ran for their cars."

"As did yours," Lance said with a grin.

"Your cover is fantastic," Betty said. "We looked into your background hard but didn't find any red flags."

"Our guys are good with cover stories," Lance said. "You're not bad yourself. I never would have pegged you as FBI."

"Thanks. Do you really surf?"

"Every chance I get," he said. "But not as much as I'd like."

"Maybe you could teach me," Betty said.

"You got it. And your first lesson can be in California in a couple of days."

"Really?" Betty said.

"Absolutely. Right after we get to his lab and wrap up the final details, we'll pose for pictures. Then I'll take you surfing."

"What?"

"Yeah, our buddy Georgio has already given me the location of where he makes the stuff," Lance said. "Haven't you, Georgio?"

"Go to hell," Georgio said, then winced and rubbed his arm.

"I think we should put Georgio in front of his lab in cuffs with us standing on either side of him," Lance said.

"I doubt if the people we work for would approve. It could blow our cover."

"It could," he said. "But the photos are for my scrapbook. Emerson loved having photos from all the golf courses he'd played. I like having at least one from each case I've worked on. It'll be something to look at in my old age when I'm sitting on the porch with my grandkids."

"What a great idea. I should start doing that," Betty said, then seemed to remember there were other people in the room. "Oh, I'm sorry. Let's see. Mr. and Mrs. Peccati, you can leave anytime you like. Chef Claire, you and Josie are also free to go. You too, Natalie."

"We're leaving in the morning," Josie said.

"Marco and Rosa, you live here," Lance said. "But just for the record, don't try to go anywhere."

"We didn't do anything," Rosa said.

"Let's hope not," Lance said.

"I could use a drink," Josie said. "You want to head into town before the circus arrives?"

"You read my mind," Chef Claire said.

"Natalie? You feel like joining us?" Josie said.

"As long as it's someplace with vodka," Natalie said, then glared down at Georgio. "I hope you rot in prison."

"I like his chances," Chef Claire said, then glanced at Marco and Rosa. "We'll see you guys later tonight or in the morning before we leave."

"I'll make breakfast," Marco said.

"What are we having?" Josie said.

"Just walk," Chef Claire said, gently shoving her toward the door. "So, will we be seeing you later, Betty?"

306

"Uh, probably not. I'll be interviewing Inspector Psycho and doing paperwork for the next couple of days. But I'll see you next time I'm back in Clay Bay."

"Which won't be long, right?" Chef Claire said.

"That would be my guess. Enjoy the rest of your trip and be safe."

"Thanks," Chef Claire said. "See you later, Lance."

"Yeah, take care," he said, waving. "May all the waves you catch be righteous."

"Whatever," Chef Claire said. "Okay, I think we better call a taxi. I have a feeling I'm going to need more than one glass of wine."

"Way ahead of you," Josie said, ending the call and putting her phone away. "Let's wait outside."

Josie waved goodbye to everyone then continued toward the door. She stopped next to Georgio who continued to gently massage his broken arm. Chef Claire also came to a stop and looked down at him.

"Sorry about your arm, Georgio," she said. "But you were trying to kill us."

"Yeah, don't worry about it. I would have done the same thing," he said.

"Why *were* you trying to kill us?" Chef Claire said.

"When things start to unravel, make sure you take care of all the loose ends," Georgio said with a shrug. He noticed Josie staring down at him. "You got something to say?"

"Thanks again for the pasta maker," Josie deadpanned.

"Bite me."

"Harsh," she said over her shoulder as she headed for the door.

Chapter 25

A little worse for wear, Chef Claire finished the last of her cappuccino and admired the view. The wind was up and producing a chop of white across the dark blue surface of the water.

"It sure is beautiful," Chef Claire said to no one in particular.

"I don't know what we'll do if we lose this place," Rosa said, following Chef Claire's eyes.

"How did Commissario Bruno react last night?" Chef Claire said.

"I don't think he was very happy," Marco said, pushing his plate away before sitting back in his chair.

"He cleared two murders and still wasn't happy?" Josie said.

"Oh, he was happy about that," Marco said. "It was the other thing that bothered him."

"Like finding out the FBI and CIA were here without anybody knowing it?" Josie said.

"Yeah, that thing," Marco said, then chuckled and shook his head.

"I take it he was angry," Chef Claire said.

"Well, if he was, he didn't show it," Marco said. "It was more like he was…what's the word I'm looking for, Rosa?"

"Resigned," she said. "He seemed resigned."

"Ah, the long arm of the U.S. government," Josie said.

"How did you leave it with Betty and Lance?" Chef Claire said.

"It sounded like they believed us when we told them we had nothing to do with what Georgio was up to. Lance was satisfied just getting his hands on him," Marco said. "But Betty might be a different matter."

"How so?" Chef Claire said.

"She said there's a possibility we could get caught up in Georgio's financial schemes if her bosses decide to go down that path," Rosa said.

"But you could fight it, right?" Chef Claire said.

"We could," Marco said. "And we'd probably try. But it would be very expensive."

"Lawyers," Josie said, shaking her head. "What a mess."

310

"The only thing that might save us is the fact the Italian government, according to Commissario Bruno, didn't know what the FBI and CIA were doing," Rosa said. "It might be enough for the Feds not to pursue the financials."

"If the Italian government starts making noises about uninvited visitors?" Chef Claire said.

"Yeah," Marco said. "Betty said her boss, some guy named Agent Tompkins, is very ambitious."

"Based on listening to her last night, she's got some serious career aspirations of her own," Josie said.

"She does," Rosa said. "And since capturing Georgio is such a huge win for the Bureau, Betty said Agent Tompkins will probably do everything he can to avoid any blowback that might taint the good publicity they're going to get."

"Blowback like the Italian ambassador going on cable news voicing his displeasure?" Chef Claire said.

"At a minimum," Marco said.

"It sounds like Betty is going to do what she can to help you out," Chef Claire said.

"I think she is," Marco said. "And if we don't have to pay back Georgio's three million, we just might make it. Especially if we sell the winery."

"Are you still thinking about putting a restaurant here?" Chef Claire said.

"We are," Rosa said. "But restaurants are so much work. And we really don't want to start working fifteen hours a day again. This was supposed to be our exit ramp into retirement."

"Yeah, the last thing we want is to get back on the freeway," Marco said.

"Find a partner who's young and hungry," Chef Claire said.

"Like you?" Marco said, raising an eyebrow.

"Not a chance," Chef Claire said, then grinned. "I'm not that young, and I'm certainly not hungry."

"I would hope not," Josie deadpanned. "You just polished off half a frittata."

"Really?" Chef Claire said, glancing over at her. "You're talking about how much *I* eat?"

"It was just an observation."

"What can I say? Capturing psychotic inventors always makes me hungry."

"Oh, good one," Josie said, nodding as she focused on Marco and Rosa. "But I think Chef Claire is onto something. Find a partner who can cook and wants to own a piece of a restaurant. It can't be that hard."

"Harder than you think," Marco said. "Especially given what happened with our last investor."

"No kidding," Rosa said. "And it could take a long time to find the right person. You know, someone we can trust."

"I'm not so sure I agree with you guys," Chef Claire said.

"You have somebody in mind?" Marco said.

"I do," Chef Claire said, then pointed across the veranda where Donato and Maria Peccati were struggling with their bags. "You've been eating their food all week, so you know how good it is. And since they're talking about opening their own place, they probably have some working capital. And they could even keep their catering operation going based out of here."

Marco and Rosa stared at each other as they gave the idea some thought.

"What do you think?" Marco said.

"It's certainly worth a conversation," Rosa said, getting to her feet and extending her arms. "Give me a hug."

She gave Chef Claire a long embrace then held her by the shoulders.

"It was so good seeing you, Chef Claire," Rosa said. "We're so proud of you. And I'm sorry about what was going on around here."

"Don't worry about it," Chef Claire said. "It could have ended a lot worse."

"But thanks to you, it didn't," Rosa said. "How the heck did you figure it out?"

"We've studied at the foot of the master," Josie said.

"Yeah," Chef Claire said. "Some of it was bound to rub off, right? Now, go talk to the Peccatis before they drive off."

Rosa glanced at Marco.

"Should we talk to them right now?"

"I don't see why not," Marco said. "Why don't you take them to the office and I'll join you in a few minutes?"

Rosa nodded then gave Josie a hug and left the veranda with a wave. Chef Claire slid an envelope across the table to Marco.

"What's this?" Marco said.

"Open it."

He did and flinched when he saw the check.

"At the risk of repeating myself, what the heck is this?"

"A little seed money to make sure the restaurant gets off to a good start," Chef Claire said.

"I thought you said you didn't want to invest."

"I don't," Chef Claire said. "Pay me back when you can."

"I can't take this, Chef Claire."

"Why not? If it weren't for you and Rosa, I wouldn't be where I am today."

"I seriously doubt that," Marco said, then glanced at the check again. "Are you sure you want to do this?"

"I am. Take the money, Marco. Don't give it a second thought."

"We'll pay you back as soon as we can."

"I know you will, Marco," Chef Claire said, getting to her feet. "But take all the time you need."

"I don't know what to say," he whispered. "Thank you, Chef Claire."

They hugged for a long time before Chef Claire let go and looked at Josie.

"Are you ready to hit the road?"

"Let's do it," Josie said, getting up from the table. "Thanks for everything, Marco."

"No, thank you, Josie," he said. "And if there's ever anything I can do, you let me know."

"Actually, there is something you can do for us," Josie said.

"What's that?"

"Let your Goldens out so we can say goodbye."

Chapter 26

"That was a sweet thing to do," Josie said, digging through her bag for her phone.

"What?" Chef Claire said, checking the rearview mirror before glancing over.

"Loaning them money."

"Oh, I'm not sure I'd call it a loan."

"What would you call it?"

"A gift," Chef Claire said. "Loans are what you get from a bank. Over the years, I've learned the hard way. When you loan money to friends or relatives, it's better to consider it a gift."

"I get that," Josie said, nodding. "It cuts down on the bad feelings if it doesn't get repaid."

"Exactly," Chef Claire said, passing a slow-moving vehicle. "Lend money to an enemy and thou will gain him. Lend to a friend and thou will lose him."

"Who said that?"

"I think it was Benjamin Franklin," Chef Claire said.

"Well, I guess Ben knew what he was talking about," Josie deadpanned. "He did end up with his face on the hundred."

"There you go."

"It was still very generous."

"Thanks."

"I'm sure they'll pay you back at some point."

"They're going to try," Chef Claire said, staring out at the highway. "And that's all that matters."

Josie located the stored number and set the phone on speaker.

"Hey, how's it going?"

"Hey, Snoopmeister. Did we wake you up?"

"No, I've been up for a while," Suzy said. "I just finished breakfast and am already thinking about what I'm going to have for lunch. I feel like I'm eating for five."

"Enjoy it while you can," Josie said.

"What's happening over there?"

"Chef Claire worked her magic last night," Josie said. "And you'll be pleased to know she was instrumental in the capture of one of the most wanted people on the planet."

"I really didn't do much," Chef Claire said. "How are you feeling?"

"I feel great. So far, pregnancy seems to be agreeing with me. You caught the guy red-handed?"

"Yeah."

"Betty must be happy," Suzy said.

"She is," Josie said. "And so is the CIA."

"What?"

"Long story," Josie said. "A very long story."

"A two bottles of wine story?" Suzy said, laughing.

"At least," Chef Claire said. "Too bad you won't be able to drink any of it while we're telling it to you."

"So, what's the deal?" Suzy said.

"We'll tell you all about it when we get home," Chef Claire said. "For now, let's just say it was a bizarre situation that fortunately ended well."

"Okay," Suzy said. "When am I going to see your next post?"

"Probably sometime tonight," Chef Claire said. "Josie's going to help me out. You know, give me her perspective on the cooking school as a non-chef."

"I am?" Josie said, glancing at Chef Claire.

"Oh, did I forget to mention it?"

"What do I need to do?"

319

"Just talk," Chef Claire said. "We'll record the conversation, and I'll just type it up later."

"I can do that," Josie said, nodding. "Will there be food?"

"We can find a quiet restaurant and do it there," Chef Claire said. "What do you feel like having for lunch?"

"Actually, I'm a little burned out on Italian food," Josie said.

"Unbelievable," Chef Claire said, laughing.

"No, I'm serious. I'm in the mood for Chinese. There must some Chinese restaurants in Milan, right?"

"Well, since several million people live there, I like our chances."

"Perfect," Josie said. "Chinese it is. Something really spicy."

"How are the dogs doing?" Chef Claire said.

"Fantastic," Suzy said. "You want to say hi?"

"No, it would only confuse them," Chef Claire said. "Just give them a hug and a kiss from me."

"Will do," Suzy said. "Where are you guys headed next?"

"We're going to spend a few days touring wineries," Chef Claire said. "I think it's time we expanded our wine list at the restaurant."

"Good call," Suzy said. "Have you come up with any new dishes?"

"I've got a bunch of ideas," Chef Claire said. "And you won't believe the bread I want to start serving."

"It's incredible," Josie said.

"I can't wait," Suzy said. "Okay, have fun, but be safe. Love you."

"Love you too," Josie said, ending the call.

She sat back in her seat and stared out the window with a small smile fixed on her face.

"Dreaming of Kung Pao chicken?"

"No, I was just thinking about something," Josie said. "We come all this way and spend our time surrounded by all sorts of amazing food."

"It was kind of the point, wasn't it?"

"Yeah, it was. But what's funny is, after all that, the thing you're most excited about is a loaf of bread."

"Bread's important," Chef Claire said. "It's essential to a good life."

"One of the staples, right?"

321

"Yeah, most definitely. If you've got good bread, you're off to a great start. It's one of those foundational things we're always talking about."

"Like having enough money to live on?"

"Yup."

"Good health."

"Absolutely."

"Family?"

"Of course."

"And the nurturing and preservation of close friendships?" Josie said, glancing over. "Like Marco and Rosa?"

Chef Claire stared out at the highway and a small smile emerged. She nodded as she glanced over at Josie.

"Yeah, that too."

Musings While I Wander

Italy in October – 4

Josie and I are sitting, as strange as it might sound, in a Chinese restaurant in Milan. But the food is good and a nice change of pace. After a week and a half of delicious Italian food, we found ourselves craving something different, yet, at the same time, something familiar. This post is the final one dealing with our week at cooking school; a week we will never forget for a host of reasons. And I've invited Josie to participate in this post to give her the chance to share her thoughts on the experience from a non-chef perspective. And as soon as she stops shoveling Kung Pao chicken down her gullet, we'll get started.

Josie – Funny.

Chef Claire – So, what was your biggest takeaway from our week at cooking school?

Josie – Apart from the need to exercise extreme caution when taking selfies?

Chef Claire – Yeah, apart from that.

323

Josie – You mean from a cooking perspective?

Chef Claire – Well, this is a food blog. So, let's start from there and see where it goes.

Josie – Okay, the biggest thing I learned is just how few ingredients are used in most dishes. Marco and Rosa kept emphasizing it's not the number of ingredients, it's the quality and freshness that counts.

Chef Claire – You were paying attention in class. Well done.

Josie – It was a little hard to miss.

Chef Claire – What else did you learn?

Josie – Probably the biggest no-no I learned was not to order a cappuccino after dinner. All the Italians looked at me like I was from another planet.

Chef Claire – Well, I'm sure you can understand their confusion.

Josie – Just so we don't get off track, I'm going to take that as a compliment.

Chef Claire - You can ask for a cappuccino at the end of a meal, but as you found out, most Italians don't.

Cappuccino is something you usually have in the morning.

Josie – There are so many rules.

Chef Claire – Actually, the Italians call them traditions.

Josie – Tomato, tomahto. But I guess it makes sense. Cappuccino is pretty heavy, especially after a big meal. One of the other things I learned is there are over 350 different types of pasta. It's a lot more than just spaghetti and lasagna noodles, huh?

Chef Claire – Indeed. And our new pasta maker handles all of them.

Josie – Thank you, Georgio. May you rot in hell.

Chef Claire – Josie's reference to Georgio isn't worth going into here, but if you'd like to know more, just keep a close eye on the news the next few weeks. What else?

Josie – Well, let's see. Oh, I know. Risotto and pasta are not considered side dishes. They are usually served as standalone items.

Chef Claire – Yes, they are. While we serve pasta as a side dish all the time, in Italy it can be a bit of a no-no.

Josie – So, I learned.

Chef Claire (laughing) – Yes, you did, didn't you?

Josie – Rosa didn't need to smack my hand with a spoon.

Chef Claire – Don't mess with mama. Especially after she's put together a multi-course meal.

Josie – That was amazing. How often do Italians eat that way?

Chef Claire – I think the full-form is done on holidays and special family celebrations. I sure wouldn't want to have to cook like that on a daily basis. Or eat like that for that matter.

Josie – Lightweight. Let me see if I can remember the order the courses come in. The first is the aperitivo, which is basically the cocktail hour. You know, drinks and a little snack.

Chef Claire – Close enough.

Josie – Then comes the antipasto which is similar to what we're familiar with.

Chef Claire – It is. Usually served cold. Cheeses, vegetables, cold cuts, some sort of bread. Some or all of the usual suspects.

Josie – I loved that bruschetta Rosa made. After that comes the first course. What's it called again?

Chef Claire – Primir. Or Primi Piatti. Which means first plate. Generally non-meat and where the pasta, risotto, or polenta are served. Or soup. It's served hot and not as heavy as the second course, but more substantial than the antipasto.

Josie – The second course is the secondi.

Chef Claire – Well done. There's no third course per se, but if there were, it would probably be called the Josie.

Josie – You're on fire today. The secondi is usually meat or fish accompanied by the contorno, a side dish of some sort of vegetable or salad, right?

Chef Claire – Yes. But the contorno is served on a different plate from the secondi. Another lesson you learned the hard way.

Josie – I was just trying to make some room at the table. It all ends up in the same place, so I don't see what the big deal was.

Chef Claire – Let's call it another of those pesky traditions. After the secondi, comes the insalata, or salad.

Josie – But if the contorno had a lot of leafy vegetables, this course might be skipped. After that comes a plate of fruit and cheese.

Chef Claire – Yes, formaggi e frutta. Regional cheeses and in-season fruit whenever possible.

Josie – Then finally we get to eat dessert. Dolce, right?

Chef Claire – Our favorite. Followed by coffee and a digestivo.

Josie – I didn't like the grappa. But the limoncello was fantastic.

Chef Claire – Grappa's not my favorite either. Hey, you did pretty good.

Josie – Thanks. And thanks again for bringing me along. It was an amazing experience.

Chef Claire – In more ways than one. Now, we tour some wineries before heading to Naples. The birthplace of pizza.

Josie – Do you really think your pizza can be improved?

Chef Claire – Without a doubt. And I'm looking forward to it. Two days working with one of the masters.

Josie (laughing) – Oh, no, not the briar patch. So, what was your biggest takeaway from cooking school?

Chef Claire – Actually, I got a lot out of it. But the best thing was learning how to make that bread.

Josie – You and your damn bread. Of all the great things you make, I still can't believe a simple loaf of bread is what gets your motor running.

Chef Claire – You'll understand it at some point.

Josie – Maybe. There was one other thing I learned.

Chef Claire – What's that?

Josie – It's something I've suspected for a long time, but last week confirmed it.

Chef Claire – Do tell.

Josie – You truly are a world-class chef.

Chef Claire – Aren't you sweet.

Josie – No, I'm serious. You could be cooking in any restaurant anywhere on earth. But you choose to stay in Clay Bay.

Chef Claire – I'm happy there.

Josie – Yeah, I get that. But still, don't you ever wonder what you might be missing out on?

Chef Claire – I did for a while. But not anymore. In fact, I'm beginning to think a month is too long to be away. I miss the dogs.

Josie – Me too. But they're in good hands.

Chef Claire – I know. And don't get me wrong, as much as I love your company, it's just not the same without having Al and Dente around.

Josie – Maybe I can help.

Chef Claire – How are you going to do that?

Josie – Woof.

Chef Claire (laughing) – Not bad. Can you do a Newfie?

Josie – Only in Italian.

www.ingramcontent.com/pod-product-compliance
Lightning Source LLC
Chambersburg PA
CBHW072125250626
47159CB00007B/2568